THE

DOOMSDAY

CLOCK:

A Reject High Legacy Novel

Brian Thompson

Copyright © 2023 by Brian Thompson

Great Nation Publishing, LLC

3826 Salem Road #56

Covington, GA 30016

www.authorbrianthompson.com

E-mail: brian@authorbrianthompson.com

ISBN: 978-0-9891056-7-5

LCCN: 2023902394

DEDICATION

This work is dedicated to the memory of Leroy Curtis Thompson.

ONE

The morning, every morning if I'm honest, greets us with belching crimson clouds and purplish-black precipitation. It has been this way since I can remember. Our air system filters the radioactive ash though the scent lingers in my nostrils. When the flurries turn acidic enough to melt skin, we stay inside and hope our shelter's protective steel and tungsten coating shields us from the atmosphere.

Except for tonight, when I stole from a forbidden sector, and it nearly cost my life.

I'd just unlatched my satchel from my shoulder when Almunashiy stirred in her compartment. She was my governess and the closest thing I had to a parent or relative. Like everyone else, she had no forename or surname, and I only called her by that title.

"What day is today, 1-13-9-18-1-8?" she asked me.

My name, my identification, was emblazoned on my temple. Everybody else called me "One" for short. Of course, there were other Ones in Sector 215 where we resided but none in my age group, gender, and certainly not my ethnicity. Almunashiy, though I'd begged her to, would not. My body stiffened whenever she called for me.

I knew the answer to her question and why she asked it—a reminder to complete my chores—but the pain in my skull after what I had done led me instead to sarcasm.

"The Doomsday Clock says it is Sunday."

She wagged her finger and sucked her teeth. "Study your political metaphors. Sharpen your wit, if you choose. But mind your tone. Do not succumb to depression."

What choice did I have? My daily routines never changed. I'd never seen beyond the dusty plains past 215's guarded boundaries.

What difference did a few letters make in the day of the week? Inside these metal confines, I study for occupations I'll never hold. And I peruse holographic images, mainly of the former world, despairing over its beauty. In my mind's eye, I can picture nothingness with ease. Never can I visualize natural light. I've never seen any. While the planet still rotates around the sun, the sun

2

itself is largely invisible. On the clearest of days, one can only catch glimpses of white brightness.

And without it, passing time meant little to nothing. Hours, days, weeks, months, years – why did it matter? Time never advanced except on 215's version of the World Clock, which I nicknamed the Doomsday Clock, for by counting forward it also counted down the time remaining until our coming demise.

More spectacle than function, its current measure was indeed twenty-two forty-five hours on Sunday, November 19, 2084.

"What have your efforts brought us this evening?" she asked. Her tone indicated neither pleasure nor displeasure. "Pulse packs? We're not due for another supply ration drop until Tuesday, and we need water."

She'd thought I'd barter with this. *Ha! I'd surprise her after all.* "Come see."

Without sunlight, everyone in the surviving four sectors would eventually die of sickness or starvation. To delay the inevitable, our people clone crops and splice protein strains and leafy greens for pulse packs to nourish us. Livestock had long been extinct, but the cloners had discovered ways to raise some vegetable species in the scorched earth.

Until the toxic rain killed them, which forced us toward the slower method of growing them inside. While waiting for a harvest, we got by on One World–provided ration packs and decontaminated water.

"Any hot particles? Why are your breaths labored. Did you run?"

I'd crouched down behind the smart garden I'd broken into, and when the droid—I didn't think to check if it was a series-R or not—started firing Ordnance, I sprinted to the exit. My sore bones ached, and the stabbing in my eyes would not relent. Also, my back stung, and I hadn't yet discovered why. I did escape that droid in the aftermath of my crime, and if it was a series-R, even if nobody escaped series-Rs, maybe I had?

"No hot particles, and yes, I ran a bit and was cautious," I fibbed. "See what I—"

"Tell me the truth so I can protect you. Did you encounter raiders, or were you stealing again?"

Even with half-truths, I had never been a convincing liar. We'd eat for a moon's cycle off what I'd gathered once it grew. Who cared about caution and the law when thievery was a misdemeanor here and not worth government intervention? Nausea bubbled in my stomach, and I became aware of my heart's rhythm at the base of my throat. Stealing in 215 meant the take was minimal. Meaning I could not lie about how I'd procured it.

"I…" My voice was higher though I did not want it to be. There was no point in salvaging my answer. The truth had been told by my silence.

She shook her head without hearing the details of my story. I'd heard rumors about the existence of radiation-resistant vegetation and proteins in adjacent Sectors 267, 454, and 610. No one dared to do anything in those places where thievery was a capital offense punishable by death.

Except me because I could. I had to look and told no one of my plans. Since 610 was the largest sector and, at twenty-six klicks away, the closest, I snuck behind its gates after dusk to discover the truth.

To *kill* me, they'd have to *catch* me. Which was difficult considering my ability to create portals and skip across distances. Each time I used it, the price was steep—a splitting headache, fatigue, bone aches, and sometimes more. I would have to pretend to be symptomless in front of Almunashiy to avoid her disapproval.

Besides, risking my life and safety on a rumor was better and more instantly gratifying than studying vegetative reproduction and completing gene-sequencing modules.

I went to my sleeping quarters to shed my hybrid weave armor. Holding it up, I noticed a singed Ordnance hole in the posterior panel flap. That explained the swelling pain in my lower back.

I'd been shot.

A glance at a reflective surface revealed a bulging, iridescent purple blotch below my kidney. A security droid, not a series-R, had tagged me with a chemical tracker, and I'd need another pair of hands to remove the hissing, bubbling skin before the robot came for me. On the plus side, I'd ask for a pain reliever, and it'd simultaneously solve both my back pain and the raging side effects of my powers.

I emptied my satchel into the hidden pantry. Almunashiy eyed me when I hesitated to straighten. She rubbed the top of her shaved head and uttered a judgmental sigh. "I raised you better than to steal from others and attempt to lie to me about it," she admonished me. "Maintain the social order at all times. There are no exceptions."

My bottom lip trembled. "I'm sorry, Almunashiy."

"Time is an undefeated warrior. Our world will end. You know this. We win battles and lose wars. At least you didn't—"

Bowing my head in reverence, I acknowledged the reminder and waved my prosthetic left hand. "No, Almunashiy. May I have an analgesic?"

She passed me by a wide margin. Never had we touched for any reason but a necessity. Never did she give a reason, and never did I ask for one. I didn't know that I

6

wanted her to embrace me, but I wanted *someone* to touch me. Her lack of kindness drew defined parameters and expectations around our partnership. A retort by me, that the social order's constructs contradicted itself, would invite punishment and a lecture about the origin of the blue numbers tattooed on our bodies.

"I raised you to be good, *the best of us,*" she said with her syringe case in her hand. Anger rippled in the air around her body. At five feet eight inches tall and ninety-seven pounds, her rangy build did not fool me. She'd dented the side of our home in anger once and suffered no ill effects. "You dodge your cloning studies, and—analgesics are expensive to trade, and we have few to spare. It wasn't worth risking being seen and tracked."

She had no idea.

"And you didn't—"

I wheezed and coughed into my fake fist. "No."

"Are you ill? Did you...?"

More than usual? "No, Almunashiy. I did not. I know the rules."

"Knowing is one thing," she reminded me. "Abiding is another. Remember this: no one who survives many nuclear winters does so on pride and impulse. No more thievery. Give me your word."

"Yes, Almunashiy."

"Your *word*. Say the words."

"I will not steal again, Almunashiy."

"Good. Now, keep your word." She always used this coda in her lectures.

After disrobing from the waist up, I lay on my night pallet. Almunashiy prepared me for a chemical peel. She'd forcefully remove the infected skin layer and incinerate it. However, we must make haste. Save for a random firestorm or electromagnetic pulse hit, once engaged, series-R droids were nearly impossible to disengage. I did not fear death as much as suffering that did not end in my death.

Soon, cool numbness spread from my midsection. I gritted my teeth while watching her through a refractive display. She unceremoniously yanked the skin free, swabbed the trickling blood, and dropped the tagged skin, swabs, and gauze in the garbage. Then, she dispatched a repurposed sentry drone to reframe my route home. The robot's energy signature would match that of the tracker and throw off a pursuer.

As she did this, I spread a patch of 3-D printed skin over the exposed area. Once the stinging eased, I knew the microorganisms had begun knitting it together with my original skin. To my left was the analgesic I'd asked for. After injecting it, I lay facedown on my pallet, closed my eyes, and let the work continue.

I awoke with a start when our illegal security protocols blared the droids' approach, which meant one of three things: nothing, torture, or execution.

I put my clothes on and covered the wound. Rather than shoot glares or order me around, my guardian hid anything incriminating. She motioned for me to do the same. I'd done so with the seeds and organic soil I'd stolen. I must remember to erect the shielding though to keep them from being found. Thinking of their intimidating titanium exoskeleton frames did not help my concentration. They broadened and lengthened to whatever size triggered adrenaline or epinephrine releases in our brains, which they could sense. The largest I'd seen was higher than eight feet. If intimidation did not work, they fired warning shots close enough to singe the hair and first layer of our skin.

I hoped to experience neither today.

We could not preempt the arrival by welcoming them inside either. Hospitality toward them incited violence. I'd done so once during a random search, and the resulting blow cracked three of my ribs.

Almunashiy and I faced one another, knelt, and crossed our arms behind our backs at the wrists. I looked down to avoid seeing her I-told-you-so glance. The chrome and black machines overrode our biometric locks and glided up to our staircase on rotating tracks.

"Remain still for identification," they said in unison.

After scanning my face and eyes, they announced my label and statistics. Five feet six inches, one hundred pounds, and a mongrel. My mixed ethnicity—Black, Asian, West Indian—meant I was part of 215's infinitesimal mongrel population. And a student. Students were anyone under twenty-one who had not been assigned a profession. I was nearly eighteen.

The other droid stated my guardian's statistics. 5-22-5. I never dared call her Five like her contemporaries. It listed her height and weight, and she was Black, too. And her occupation was technocrat. *Her, a technocrat?* I fought a smile. Her lie was more egregious than mine. Cloning was illegal, but lying to machines to survive was different than wanting to skip a lecture. We traded for all our technology and called on 23-9-12-12, a fellow cloner but mechanically inclined, during malfunctions. Almunashiy couldn't rewire a simple switch. Nor could I.

These droids were supposed to operate on unbiased programming, but they didn't. Our race and ethnicity earned us the worst treatment. Made me wonder why Almunashiy created me as a mongrel. She knew the trouble I would face with straight teeth and bushy hair...if I let it grow. The advances in somatic cell nuclear cloning made doing so a simple selection as long as both the egg cell and body cell were viable.

Though the genetic source material would've cost her a fortune, she could've made me Caucasian with thin, fine hair. Then, I'd have lived healthily in the better sectors like 267, which, from what I'd heard, had the lowest radioactive charge of the four remaining areas. I would not be a starving mongrel living here, but I would have been alone since no one with Black ancestry lived there. My creator might not show me warmth, but she was always present.

The lines in Almunashiy's face...she questioned whether I'd erected the secret pantry's uranium shielding. My chest tightened. I couldn't recall. Since the droids' algorithms calculated facial and biological reactions, I cleared my mind to avoid tipping my hand. Should they discover the seeds, they would waste no time spilling our blood.

Following their scans in our kitchen, they did nothing. Strange. The compartment's position in our trailer was supposed to make it appear to be a normal piece of composite shielding against excessive radiation spikes. I must have shut it after all.

Once they had completed looking, the machines left. I engaged the locks, reset the defense systems, and freely breathed. "Guess the crime rate rose above forty-five percent, huh?"

"Hmm. Maybe. Or they were looking for you."

My mentor resumed her surly disposition. She accessed the secret compartment and palmed the collection with wonder. Holding the clear packages up to the hanging light fixture, she shook them and marveled at the brown and white contents.

"Impossible."

I shook my head. *Possible*.

We went to the greenhouse compartment where Almunashiy had replicated a non-hostile fertile environment. All the best cloners had one, and none of them were abundantly fruitful. Thieves avoided them entirely. Seeds did not render quick results.

Temperature control and natural sunlight were simple to reproduce. Potable water was expensive in trade but easy enough to procure. The fertile soil was the biggest obstacle. There weren't many places left to grow food though the package I'd stolen was proof the wealthy had solutions they kept to themselves.

Almunashiy dug her hands into a pot of crumbled, burnt earth and set the soil from the package on the top. She dropped in a couple of seeds, covered them up, and watered them from a cup. Normal vegetative growth should take weeks. Here, in seconds, three plants sprouted buds. Perhaps now, we could reverse engineer the science together and surpass the life expectancy rate of forty years. I suspected Almunashiy was close.

"When the droids were here," I said with a sense of dread, "could not I have tried—"

"Not worth the price of failure." Her answer was short, forceful. She passed her hand across the silver metal worktable to me. Underneath it were protein ration packets I'd stolen a while ago. "We need more water. Go to the Hub. Finish your bartering by midnight before the night sweeps. I will start the compound's descent into the ground in that time."

A two-klick round trip in less than thirty minutes without cheating did not allow much space for error, but being caught by a security droid would be much worse. She would lower our home underground for the night, and I would have to use my powers and guess my way inside it. There would not be further discussion between us, and trading for supplies *was* among my list of Sunday chores.

I donned my protective gear and water collection tank, holstered an Ordnance and a knife, and left the compound.

My stomach rumbled. I would eat when I returned.

Outside, violent winds ripped across my covered body and goggles. At sector 215's heart was the Hub, a trading post where we socialized about our shared misery and pooled our resources. Monetary units were practically useless without a functioning economy to support them. So, bartering earned us clothing, food, potable water—whatever we needed. Raiders were always present, which is why I never went unarmed. I preferred knives because my shooting left much to be desired, but one needed to be close to stab someone, and I could easily be overpowered.

The seeds I'd stolen would've been worth a fortune had I offered them in trade, but there was no way to do so without explaining what they were or revealing where I'd gotten them from. The reward for someone turning me in as a traitor would be hefty.

I hated when Almunashiy was right.

The service droid at the bar poured me a cup of purified water, filled the dispersal container on my back, and paused for payment. I gave the multi-protein packets to it. The water supply would last us through tomorrow if we bathed, days longer if we didn't.

As I leaned against the structure to support the added weight to my frame, 8-1-18-12-15-23 joined me. Eight and I had nothing in common. Beady-eyed and intrusive, she considered me a best friend. True, we'd known one another since early childhood, but I did not consider us more than passing acquaintances. Life in a nuclear wasteland was a survival competition. Anyone succeeding too well became a target.

Her gravelly voice was piqued with interest. "You heard about 610? The burglary in the senator's home?"

Feigning believable ignorance about what I'd done was key, which was not difficult since I did not know it was the home of a politician. "That is suicidal."

She swallowed her water all at once, tapped the glass bottom on the splintered pine surface, and wiped her head with a grease-stained white cloth. Taller than me and Almunashiy but just as slender, Eight leaned in close enough for me to smell protein on her breath. "I keep telling you to wear a smartwatch, so you'd know these announcements when they are made. Somebody made off with a moon cycle's worth of enhanced seeds. If I had a death wish, I'd have attempted it myself."

Her backhanded compliment flattered me, but I did not seize the temptation to gloat. "You are impressed?"

"No one I've ever known would do something that risky and stupid."

Risky, yes, but stupid? I was offended but still needed to cover myself. "What is the reward?" My dried mouth was painful. "Split it with you if I hear anything."

Eight clicked her teeth. "You'll keep your mouth shut unless you want your head blasted in like Twenty-Three."

My jaw dropped. *Twenty-Three was dead?* "When?"

"The machines found ashes of a chemical tracker in a reprogrammed droid wandering near his trailer, and get

15

this, *a droid tagged the seed thief.* Must've been him. Executed him on the spot."

I choked back tears and regretted what I'd accomplished. Almunashiy and he shared a special bond I did not understand. Unlike Almunashiy, he had a life mate. An innocent man had died for what I had done, and the truth about it would never be known. Such was the filthy nature of totalitarian government propaganda in our state. He'd be cremated, and his ashes would be tossed away like refuse. Left to depend on her rations alone, his life mate would starve.

But the lesson, *do not steal from us,* would be well learned.

My skin grew clammy, and I'd lost the desire to keep what I'd stolen since I'd traded a friend's blood to get it. A gaze at the Doomsday Clock above us told me I had violated curfew by three minutes. The sweeps had begun and would not finish for hours. Everyone would wait them out until the next watch, which I might now have to do. I swallowed hard. Unlike my friend, at least I'd get the chance.

Eight patted me on the shoulder. She must have interpreted my building grief as depression. "Get home. Use your water wisely, young one. We're on lockdown. Nothing in or out of the borders."

"For how long?"

16

Her black eyes focused down. No one knew.

Then, the intent of the supply blockade must not be for us to survive it. Starving the most impoverished sector was cruel in its poeticism. It was then I noticed the stares. As I stood, the liquid loudly sloshed on my back. My collection container was full. Theirs were not. The bar had shut down after accommodating a handful of us, most of whom were female.

Suddenly, we were carrying a fortune in survival goods and flaunting it. Raider men had already approached the other water carriers. One to my far left had her neck snapped. A girl my size across the room collapsed, her throat slit. A brawl ignited in the area's center that conveniently blocked the exit.

My shoulders dropped. Escaping would be simple for me. Not for Eight. Unless I told her, which I had been forbidden to do.

Might as well fight.

"You armed?" she asked me.

Hand near my holster, I nodded. Had I known about these developments, I would have never come to the bar, which was at the rear of the trading post.

Good thing Eight was here. Even side by side, with her a much better marksman than me, the two of us couldn't blast our way to safety unharmed.

Eight handled her Ordnance at my eye level and flipped its setting from stun to kill. "Stay close."

TWO

Tingling ebbed through my fingers. Almuashiy's midnight curfew, which I'd now broken, came to mind. Being "good" and earning her approval was everything to me.

Tonight, I'd disappoint her again.

With my prosthetic hand, I yanked Eight by the wrist and cocked my head to indicate the direction in which we should run before shooting began. Together, we hustled through the owner's exit and into the open air. My skin protested the wind's needling bite. *My mask!* I had left it on the counter. I had my goggles, though, and I needed them to properly see through the darkness. "How long can you hold your breath?" I asked her while backing against a compound's exterior wall.

"What?" she mouthed.

Although we could barely see and hear one another, we knew raiders were closing in on us. I unlatched the water container and left it on the ground. Once we moved, those following us ignored it.

Did they want something else: our clothes, supplies? Failing that, *our bodies?* I'd never considered myself female except in this regard. Coitus was a messy, disgusting process. With childbirth mortality a near certainty, nobody engaged in sex for reproduction, just for entertainment or crime. Somatic nuclear cloning was imperfect—the need for my prosthetic left hand was proof of that—but a more direct, effective method to create life.

The process would not stop our attackers. They yelled all the vile things they'd do to us and laughed. I'd heard raiders stab one another in nonlethal places for fun. My armor could absorb knife blows and Ordnance, too, except kill shots. Stripping off my armor without the know-how and biometric access to its locks would take minutes.

I'd fight, back-to-back with Eight, until I...*we*...could escape.

Cornered behind a rusted storage trailer, I confessed enough of the truth to gain Eight's trust. "I can get us out of here."

"Really? *How?*"

She needed more information, which meant I had to break Almunashiy's second most-sacred rule and tell my secret. "I have...*an ability.*"

She tightly clutched her Ordnance's handle and fired a few shots around the trailer. By the heavy, weighted thuds and yells I'd heard, she'd taken down two of our pursuers. With the winds blowing hard enough to move the goggles on my face, how did it not alter her aim?

"Sure, you do," she mocked. "Look, we'll scare them off. There's only four left."

Four raiders who knew our approximate position. I'd have to show her. Eight would believe it when she saw it.

I beckoned her with my fake hand to stay close. No one else besides her needed to know. We'd have a brief window to escape once I opened the route.

And then?

Almunashiy would be livid I had shown another living being. I'd never known how I came to be this way but, with my good hand, I could open a gate to cross a distance. I'd never navigated the bridge between where I had left and where I was going with anyone, not even my guardian. Almunashiy's theory was that I'd subconsciously constructed a safe place—a waystation inside a wormhole. I called it the Narrow Space. Each time put me at risk of asphyxiation and being crushed to a pulp by gravity, and Eight would be at further risk with me.

Presently, it was our only chance.

I gestured for her again to stay close. Irritated, she waved me away.

Ordnance shots pinged and sizzled against our cover from the rear. The raiders were out to spill blood. Although our domicile had already been searched once tonight, I could not help thinking that, like Twenty-Three, Almunashiy was dead—bloodied and lying on our compound floor or blown away in a coarse pile of bombed-over ash.

I focused on the destination, pictured it in my mind—our land plot's eastern border behind the compound—and stretched out my arm. By now, Almunashiy would have buried the compound underground for the night to shield against nightly radioactivity spikes. Hopefully, the energy twisting and surging inside me and tingling up to my fingertips would deliver us there.

I felt an excruciating stab in the nerves of my left wrist's stump. My prosthetic's wiring translated the power as electrical impulses, like electrocution on a smaller level. I tasted metal sparks. This happened to me every time like an invisible judgment against a deformity I had no control over. I struggled with losing my temper, tossing the thing into an incinerator, and living as a proper amputee.

Eight elbowed me in the arm and pointed. "What is *that?*"

The ice-blue circle of light the size of my clenched fist? Yes, I saw it. Spreading my fingers widened it enough for us to step through. "A way out." I nodded. "I created it."

In the blue glow, behind her goggles' dirty glass, I saw Eight's eyes bulge. She turned her back to me and returned fire. "You're one of *those?*" she spat out. "Nobody thought the vigilante stories were real!"

I nodded. I'd seen the old reports and film of masked people doing incredible things, but I had not identified as one until discovering my abilities in my early teens. "They're real. I'm *real.*"

"Yeah, well, I don't just walk through supernatural doors."

Which meant I'd have to force her close enough for the gravitational pull to suck her in. I'd need to knock the wind out of her first. Otherwise, the oxygen in her lungs would expand and kill her. My stomach clenched. A miscalculation could end her; however, I must try.

Without warning, she dropped to the ground beside me, slumped over in my lap, a gaping crater burned through the right eye socket. A bloody, smoking lump of gore from the fatal wound oozed onto the ground between my knees.

I thrashed my legs to free myself from the dead weight. Since I'd unclenched my fist at the sight of Eight's corpse, the portal had closed on itself. And when I looked up, two raiders emerged from the darkness and pointed their Ordnance barrels at me. Without warning, I fell through the ground into a dark pit. Just as quickly, I dropped out of its bottom and landed hard on my tailbone.

I found myself outside our land plot's eastern border. Strange. Exactly where I had planned? It was long after curfew, and Almunashiy hadn't begun the compound's descent sequence. At its quickest setting, the process might take ten minutes. The entrance ramp lowered, and I heard the rhythmic cadence of mechanical voices.

We'd been searched...*again?*

With my back to the rear wall, I tried to suppress the rise and fall of my chest and think past my throbbing skull as well. Saliva gathered at the back of my throat. I lifted my mask, spat away from the wind as quietly as possible, and lowered it again. I'd never used two portals so close together and braced myself for more physical anguish. The headache swelled, as expected, and I felt close to losing consciousness.

The droids' mechanized gears hummed louder as they rolled to the ground without incident and motored away. I'd pause for a few moments until they were out of listening range. I counted to three hundred and repeated it twice.

Soon thereafter, the ramp lowered again, and I heard a human descending it. This was familiar—the crusted soil's texture beneath my soles, the burnt stench in the

24

air. I'd been in this place before almost like I remembered... *Had I dreamed it?* For unexplainable reasons, I knew not to confront the human. I'd approach my home after he or she left.

I suspected Almunashiy had been the one to exit the compound, and I'd prefer not to face her wrath, but I circled to the front. She blocked the entrance to our home looking outward.

Her countenance dropped at the sight of me, and the color drained from her face. If she was here, then who had left—a fellow cloner?

Before I could ask, Almunashiy drew her weapon.

I froze, unable to speak, tears welling in my eyes. My limbs trembled. Would she kill me then? Her eyes flitted back and forth between me and the space beyond me like she was contemplating which one of us to kill. She aimed in my general direction. Her Ordnance's scope light flashed and blinded me. I closed my eyes so I'd never see it coming.

I heard the shot's crack and high-pitched sizzle.

Seconds later, I did not think I'd died. I did not experience a fatal level of agony, just the residue of my abilities. I came to the realization I was still in front of my home. Almunashiy had disappeared. Soon, she passed on my right side dragging a facedown human body toward me by its ankle. She had murdered before. Lengthy survival in these times required a kind of remorseless brutality, Almunashiy would say, but she hadn't ever done so in front of me. She dropped the body's right leg with a thud and retreated into the building.

My quivering limbs warned me to remain rooted to the spot. Sweat dampened my chest. A female or a slightly-built man...the body's identity was a mystery to me. I eyed the empty water collection tank on its back. Funny. The pressure sensor had a dent shaped like a crescent moon on the lower right side *just...like...mine.*

I approached the lifeless body. The closer I drew, the bigger the sense of dread in my bones and the more my leg muscles tightened. My suspicions weren't humanly possible. Still, I must know. The armor's design resembled mine down to the abrasions on the leg side panels. I touched the flanks on my own and imagined the small fissures from wear were identical as well. The body would be too heavy for me to roll over alone. The barbarous entry wound was precise—at the base of the neck.

Kneeling beside its upper thigh, I put my hand on the collection tank and lifted it an inch or so to squeeze my good hand beneath it. In the darkness, I couldn't tell if there was a hole in the rear panel, but I'd be able to feel it if there was. I had no clue what I'd do if that were the case. The potential repercussions of what I thought overwhelmed me.

26

Right when I slid my hand beneath the tank, Almunashiy reemerged with a silver globe the size of a human head. "Don't!" she roared.

I'd seen the globe once—a reductor. We owned two. Their primary function was rapid corporeal decomposition. There was one for each of us since belowground burial was not prudent and proper cremation cost too much.

I quickly retreated from the body before she pressed her palms on either side of the machine, held on until it glowed bright green, and threw it at the corpse. The instrument vaporized everything in its vicinity, including an inch or so of dirt, and I held my breath while the black smoke dissipated. No need to inhale human remains even if they were leveled down to particles. This was the only way series-R droids could not detect human DNA, but the extent of their evolving capabilities were mysteries until we saw them.

Almunashiy grabbed my arm, and my limb seized. "Come, 1-13-9-18-1-8."

Unaware I had been whimpering, I bit my lip trying to hold back the rush of emotion inside and ended up pushing it outward in sobs and nonsense. She checked me for wounds and, finding none, urged me into the compound.

A few moments passed before my stiff legs, still locked at the knees, slowly moved forward. I followed my mentor

27

into the compound before she could become irritated with my feelings and shut me outside for the night. From her hasty movements to lock the compound down, I could tell I had indeed annoyed her or, perhaps, provoked another emotion I'd never encountered from her or rarely seen. I'd done my best to obey her at all times, and invariably, I'd failed in spots. But tonight, I wasn't even clear on what I'd done to irk her so badly or why she'd murdered someone in cold blood.

"Almunashiy?" I said barely above a whisper.

She paused at the controls and did not look at me. "Do you see the time?"

No. She knew I didn't. I never did. "It's after curfew," I said a bit louder, "and the compound should be underground. I will clean hot particle residue every morning for a week, but this, all of this—it's not because of me, and I—"

"Is it not? Do you see the time?"

"N-no."

Almunashiy rummaged through my quarters and found a rectangular case I'd hidden. Inside it was the smartwatch I had worn once or twice at her insistence. She forced it into my hand. Her brown eyes normally warmed me with acknowledgment I interpreted as affection, but the way they glared at my goggled eyes now did not indicate she was pleased. I was thankful she could not see my tears. I'd be paying closer attention to the passing of time from now on whether I liked it or not.

I opened the container and latched the black smartwatch with gray straps to my wrist although it needed adjusting. According to its reading, curfew hadn't passed. It was about ten minutes away, and the date wasn't right either. That didn't make sense. The batteries on these things were supposed to last *years,* and it was practically unused. I started toward the cabinet where we kept the replacement battery cells.

Almunashiy stopped me and pointed toward the time on our home's display. The date and time were exactly the same as my smartwatch.

"You haven't checked the Doomsday Clock since your return." Almunashiy's voice shook. "What day is today, 1-13-9-18-1-8?"

My entire body quivered. November 18, 2084, twenty-three thirty hours. What does this mean? What had happened to me?

"How did you do it?" she asked me.

I tried to speak and could not. How did I do *what?*

"You reversed time dilation, inverted your wormhole's gravitational pull, sustained the event horizon, broke the second law of thermodynamics—"

The scientific words spilling from her mouth made little sense to me. I wondered if my frozen eyes

29

communicated to her how crazed I felt. "Eight..." I mouthed.

"8-1-18-12-15-23? Did she see your portal?"

I nodded. But she'd died.

Although she appeared relieved no one else knew about me, Almunashiy paced the floor and asked me questions more quickly than I could answer them. *When did Eight die, before or after the raiders cornered us? At what time? Was the portal any different than the others I'd ever conjured?*

After. I don't know. Only that I fell through it instead of being drawn inside.

"Again, how did you manipulate the time dilation to skip across realities? What about entropy, negentropy—"

Wait.

When I'd escaped the portal a few minutes ago, droids were *leaving*.

Almunashiy's guest carried a water collection container *identical to mine*.

She'd killed someone appearing to be me *and vaporized the remains*.

I held my hand up and walked to the furthest end of the compound which, truthfully, was not more than two yards. My heart dropped in mourning as if to say goodbye to a piece of myself. Almunashiy had never done anything

30

to intentionally harm me, and then, she'd done the worst although it hadn't directly harmed me, had it? Had it?

Physically, I felt no different. But mentally, I suddenly wondered about what I hadn't even considered prior to this. Her nature to violently eliminate threats extended to me. Perhaps it always had, and I'd been wholly ignorant. To steady my balance and to stop shaking so much, I sat on the floor and used my arms to pull my knees to my chest.

Still, I'd give her the chance to explain, which, from the extended silence between us, she seemed reluctant to do. Once the compound fully descended underground for the night, she'd be a captive audience, and I'd press for answers. Until then, I'd contemplate the ramifications of what I'd accomplished. My studies had not covered quantum physics and theoretical time travel, and now that time travel was no longer theoretical, I had an urge to understand and control what I could suddenly do.

What were the rules of *this* ability? Everything in my life had boundaries, techniques, procedures, and the like. This had to be no different.

The resting hiss of the hydraulics indicated the burial process had finished. We'd remain here for the next two night watches, six hours, which gave us plenty of time to talk. There would be no rest for me unless I gained an understanding of what I'd done and what was happening to me. My limbs trembled again, and I struggled to stop them.

"Almunashiy?" My quaking voice broke. The second time I beckoned her, she appeared in her quarter's entryway and sat on my pallet facing me. The distance between us was palpable, but I could still hear her throaty voice.

She inhaled, took out her holographic pen, and drew a white line with an arrow at the end and a large square with two dots on opposite sides in the air. She labeled it time, pinched the display, and rotated it so I didn't have to read backward.

"Up until today," she said, "you understood time only flows forward, like this line. You exited your former reality, where Eight died, and you entered this current reality, where Eight is still alive and at the Hub right now."

"I reversed time?"

Her finger drew an angled line perpendicular to the one labeled time. "In a way. You left your timeline and created a branched reality."

A solitary thought came to mind in the first lucid moment I had since falling through the portal. Almunashiy's face was ashen more so than usual, and she looked in my direction, not at me, but *through* me. I'd never seen this reaction in her before.

She was afraid.

THREE

D id she fear me or what I'd done? What I'd
become?

Or something else?

Rather than share her apprehensions with me, which she had never done, Almunashiy prattled on about the timeline I had broken and this new reality I'd fashioned. The more I focused on what she was saying, I noticed her words were *about* me and not directed *to* me. Most of them were pronounceable nonsense, but they impacted me like a wild, unplanned fist. I hadn't intended to do what I'd done—ended Eight and Twenty-Three's lives and possibly reversed the former—but my well-meaning intent did nothing to resuscitate them. They'd always be dead in some reality because of me.

Their blood dripped from these impulsive decisions, and the regret of my mistakes chewed at my soul like rabid vermin. By the way she hid her face from me, it was obvious the news of her friend's death had emotionally affected her.

My voice quivered. "Can I restore the original timeline?"

In her words, no. I'd laid the prime timeline, whatever that was, to waste and couldn't repair it unless I was willing to go back, not change anything, and let Eight, Twenty-Three, and myself die, which neither of us was. From her tense holographic scribbling that followed, and the way Almunashiy pursed her thick pink lips, she was sure of this; although up until this moment, she believed negentropy—reversing the disorder I'd released—was impossible.

Everything would always be different and stay different, thanks to me.

I had not ruined many things in my life mostly because I feared attempting anything. And I had not meant to do what I'd done in the first place. I'd apparently just been too afraid of my head getting blasted.

Writing in a frenzy, she continued repeating herself, "What you did is..." She continued to babble about inverted portals and negentropy across the planet.

"Almunashiy, I am sorry. I—"

The more she explained things, the more confused I became until she waved her index finger in front of my face. "There must be entropic balance. Two of you cannot exist at the same time. It's chaotic displacement with consequences I cannot quantify."

I understood so little, and I was a fool to think whatever I'd thought.

Her drawing's linear concept was simple enough, but its nature evoked questions I did not feel enough freedom to vocalize. My head throbbed. The ensuing silence between us was bothersome. Even the wind outside had calmed itself.

After clearing my throat, I went to move my lips, but I had lost the nerve to speak. Had I dedicated myself to studying advanced science more than English, I might have understood her explanation beyond its basic diction. Instead, my questions would be considered wrong, inappropriate, asinine, *obvious*.

One thing remained, though, and I did not have to bring it up.

She had not killed me, she reiterated, but she'd eliminated an entropic duplicate I'd created by journeying within my own lifetime. "Again, two versions of you must *never* coexist," she said while starting the compound's descent sequence.

I shouted over the humming and hissing, "But Almunashiy, *the lockdown!* Shouldn't we—"

"You embolden yourself to backtalk me? Nothing can change that now," she bellowed. "There is no water to be had. That problem will not solve itself before morning."

We'd spend tonight underground, thirsty, encased below twenty feet of dirt, until morning when the hot particle levels were safer. Then, once we reemerged, we'd eat and drink what we had left and be dead in less than a week.

Not that it mattered. Without a supply delivery, everyone in 215 would soon be brittle skeletons anyway.

I went to my pallet determined to rest and not think about the person I'd trusted more than anyone shooting any version of me.

The wetness on my cheek indicated I'd slept for some amount of time—how much, I was not sure. Finding a comfortable position was a challenge. Then, there was the matter of the flickering lights. Once those darkened, the air filtration's intermittent rattle did it, and then, the *silence*. Oh, the sound of nothing! I assumed Almunashiy slept, but I'd never seen her close to nodding off, and her compartment was too far away for me to peek into. So much of her humanity was a mystery to me. Had I not grown used to her moldy scent, I'd think she did not sweat either.

I assumed my post in front of the oval windows and anticipated the compound's ascension to the surface. My anticipation built with the rhythm beat by our home's gradual rise. The mud clumps and tiny water bubbles sliding down the glass settled my nerves.

I ate my last protein packet and watched the process. As I did, a sharp point pricked my ribs. I looked down. Almunashiy had poked a rectangular box into my midsection. In it was the black and gray holographic smartwatch with metal wrist straps I'd taken off before I slept and hoped she had forgotten about.

After last night's events, I didn't get the impression I was being given a choice. I'd eschewed wearing anything time related for a number of reasons, but my actions earned these limits for me. I latched it on to my left wrist above my prosthetic's bond and stared at it—another limitation to weigh me down. A portable Doomsday Clock.

"Time is a feeble construct," I muttered to myself.

"A finite construct," she corrected me, "and it warrants your utmost respect, especially now."

Did it though? I'd never argue with her out loud. But should I respect an ancient mathematical equation that evolved from sundials and devolved back to its origins? Without daylight and different seasons, the concept of weeks, days, hours, minutes, and seconds was pointless. There were no planting times, harvests, holidays, or celebrations. Why measure time? For tradition? Every day was the same. The longer we chronicled it, the closer we arrived to our deaths.

Who needed to be reminded of mortality every second of every day?

Near the end of the compound's noisy reemergence cycle, I noticed a set of human feet through the windows. Almunashiy did as well. How could anyone know where we lived? Curiosity piqued my interest more than anything, and as I pointed and commented out loud, I noticed tiny sweat beads on her forehead. We'd been belowground for the duration of the evening, and I'd never have called our living space's atmosphere more than temperate during an energy conservation cycle.

No, she knew this person and feared them.

She directed me to go to her quarters, and I obeyed without hesitation. I'd never been alone in her quarters since my childhood. The rectangular confines had to be better than my small personal area.

And indeed, they were despite the rusted metal walls badly needing reconditioning. Besides that, it was spacious. Her pallet's padding was uncomfortable, like mine, and the purplish-gray covers were filthy and threadbare. Her clothing, strewn across the floor in unkempt wads, held no mysteries. We did not entertain visitors often.

I glanced at the disorganized shelves. Most of the tech escaped my scope of understanding, and the labeled learning modules—string theory, chaos theory, metaphysics, quantum mechanics, nuclear fusion and fission... *Ugh.* Science had its worth, but all kinds of literature, even history, spoke to my soul. I had an imagination beyond the every day because of it.

My entire life, Almunashiy had begged me to show interest in eugenics, gene therapy, and cloning, and I couldn't interest myself in her life's work.

Perhaps someday.

The compound's hydraulic locks shifted into place. Our guest, should Almunashiy allow them, would enter our home, and I'd witness the full conversation via holographic surveillance display.

"Hello, Nazirah."

I relied on paltry lip-reading skills and a low volume to eavesdrop. Nazirah was the darkest-skinned human being I'd ever seen, hauntingly contrasted against her sparkling white teeth. A wispy skeleton of a woman, she wore an assortment of tattered brown rags from the neck down. Black braided hair cascaded down her back, and she had a forename. Not numbers. A name. Prior to the status quo, the population had forenames and surnames. What was her surname?

Nazirah's voice was steady and worn with a subtle, foreign accent.

She looked in my general direction, greeted Almunashiy, and said two words that froze my blood.

"It's time."

Time for what? Though Nazirah did not specifically mention me, the manner in which Almunashiy stiffened her posture implied it involved me. How did Nazirah know I was back here in this room? Had she come here before? I knew the faces of practically every adult in 215, and I would have remembered her.

My muscles tightened. Before last night, when I'd seen Almunashiy assassinate my entropic duplicate, I believed she'd protect me against all threats. Now, I was not certain. Nazirah was here about me, and I had to take care of myself.

Though I'd always suspected Almunashiy was a pacifist from her unflappable demeanor, I rummaged through her belongings for the Ordnance she'd fired the night before, and finding none, I looked for a means to defend myself. All my blades were with my belongings, and her room had nothing sharper than a lightweight, wide-handled, blunt tool that might badly bruise someone if I attacked with all the force I could muster. Still, I

40

clutched it, hoping it would be enough in an emergency situation.

"You must come with me to Vagrant City." She winced as she sat. "Don't make me fight you over this."

Almunashiy pursed her lips. "Please. You couldn't defeat me on your best day."

Nazirah chuckled. "The commission has long been completed. You cultivated the strand and grew it into what was needed. The time has now come for it to serve its purpose."

Looking away, Almunashiy said nothing.

The it was *me*.

Nazirah nodded, and said, "Oh, so it already has! How long do you imagine you have until the government is at your doorstep and discovers your success?"

My insides boiled, and I clutched the instrument in my right hand. I'd brain her if she referred to me as a thing again.

"They would not bother," Almunashiy said. "We are all about to die of starvation."

"Then, you'd rather die here, with your charge, than come with me? You cannot hate me that much."

Almunashiy called me by identification number, and I lost my nerve. Accidentally dropping the silver instrument on my feet, I lowered my head and walked toward them.

Nazirah's posture was stooped, but she still stood a head above us both. She cradled my chin and lifted my head so that we were eye to eye. Nazirah had darkened blood clots in her eye sclera and scattered keloids all over her cheeks and temples.

"My name is Nazirah, *bint*. What are you called?"

"*Bint*?"

"*Bint* is Arabic for daughter," Nazirah replied.

I nodded, and after I said my numbers, she sucked her teeth. She expected me to have a forename, like her. The One World government had outlawed their use to better identify and classify survivors though it served to dehumanize us as well. Her rough finger pads lingered on my face long enough for awkwardness to set in. Then, she told me the same thing she'd told Almunashiy in not so many words—we would go to a place called Vagrant City where I was needed.

"Needed for what?" I blurted out. "To serve my purpose?'"

"Indeed. For the Omnikhron you generate," she said

"The–"

"What you can do, the portals, they're called Omnikhron from the Greek omni meaning all and khronos meaning time. This is the very reason for which you were created. You need training, however, to gain control over them."

42

The distance- and time-bending portal had a name, *Omnikhron,* but I didn't? And if it had a name, it had a history whereas I did not know my own. My caretaker had never disclosed anything about her background or mine, and now, I was intrigued. Could I have a past beyond being a matured collection of cells? Could Nazirah decode the mysteries of my life?

"Control? To do what?"

She extended her hand. "Come with me, and we will find the answers together."

"We will not make it past the border with the lockdown," I said. "There will be a droid army."

"Pack weapons and clothes for two days' travel. Just the essentials," she said to us. "Leave the border and droids to me."

My shoulders dropped. Two days' travel sounded like an eternity. I had never gone that far away except for 610, and I had cheated the distance through a wormhole or Omnikhron. What a strange word!

While Nazirah explored our makeshift greenhouse, I quietly spoke to Almunashiy. "Do you trust her?"

She paused while collecting small items out of my sight line. "I used to."

"Is she telling the truth about training me and everything?"

"Yes," she said without hesitation. "This time, we must do as she says."

Essential for me was simple—rations and some protection. We had no water left. As for weapons, there were my knives and Ordnance sidearm. I pocketed all the cartridges of backup ammunition I had.

I hated blades, but I was adept in using them. I stuck them in my boot holsters. I couldn't lift the 3D skin printer or the recommissioned droid, but I pocketed antiseptic spray and radiation burn salve from the medic kit and shouldered two empty canteens.

After stuffing clothes into my supply pack, I donned my armor. Would I see my home again? In case I wouldn't, I tore off a piece of my purplish-gray blanket I had an unreasonable attachment to and tied it around my leg. Then, I declared myself ready. I must've weighed an extra five pounds from all the additional gear.

Almunashiy presented five of our last protein rations and demanded I eat them. "You will not survive the journey if you do not eat," she warned.

Hearing that, I obliged and drank the dregs of one of my canteens. She was right. Trekking to the border, even at this time of morning, would take a good deal of energy, and we'd need water first thing. Trading for it was impossible, and provided we passed the droid blockade, we'd never make it beyond the reservoir without it.

Almunashiy must have been working from a mental list. Her supply pack was full and looked heavier than I could hope to lift. She hefted it on her back as if it were nothing though she and I were comparable in size. For most of my life, I wondered about the source of her extraordinary strength and its exact limits.

Maybe we were about to find out.

"We will go to the reservoir first," Nazirah said. "I know that is of some concern."

My eyes bulged behind my goggles. Nothing could have prepared me for a twelve-klick hike first thing in the morning. A key to maintaining a semblance of health and sanity in 215 was avoiding increased exposure to outside air and the debris it carried. Inside the compound, our filtration system dealt with the environmental hazards and toxins. How would we survive without it?

Out in the open, Almunashiy and I breathed through our masks while Nazirah proceeded unbothered and spit out black lumped particles she'd inhaled. She secured the compound, and as we started in the direction of the reservoir, someone appeared in the distance.

"Who is approaching?" she asked. "Are they friend or foe?"

Almunashiy and I adjusted our goggles' visual displays to zoom. "That's an acquaintance of 1-13-9-18-1-8," she said. "Her name is 8-1-18-12-15-23. They know each other."

She lived! "Will Eight join us?" I asked with a smile. "She is the best marksman I've ever seen, and she could take out series-R droids guarding the water half a klick away."

I blinked, and the next thing I knew, Eight appeared next to me in a cloud of foul-smelling green smoke. She unmasked, vomited clear liquid on the ground, and cursed. While I was glad to see her alive, her appearance raised more questions than it answered.

Before I could ask if she was an entropic duplicate, Nazirah said, "Arm yourselves, hold your breath, and close your eyes."

Immediately, we reached the reservoir. The green smoke dissipated, and Nazirah, who must've been the one moving us across distance, bent over and gasped. Almunashiy waved her Ordnance trying to assess the threat level.

Except there didn't seem to be one.

Eight cursed and asked questions. Tears welled in my eyes. I wanted to embrace her since the last time I'd seen her she had a sizable hole blown in her head. When no one answered her inquiries at first, it looked as if she might run, but she said the immediate uncertainty of what she might be running into by leaving us might be worse. Eight's presence should have put me at ease but did not. In addition to dealing with everything else, now I worried whether or not I had put her at risk simply by identifying her.

I'd never seen the reservoir in person. From ground level, it looked to be an incline that dipped into a reflective pool. No series-R droids guarded the clear biodome covering it like we thought they would. Only the rail-thin maintenance droids were left to manage the underground reserves. This contradicted what I'd learned about our supply chain that the reservoir was supposedly full of water farther than the eye could see and heavily guarded.

Of course, now, I appeared foolish for including Eight. We did not need her skills as immediately as I thought.

"What happened?" I asked out loud.

Eight gave voice to what we were all thinking. "Who are you?" she asked Nazirah. "Where's all of the water? There can't be more than a two-week supply for all the zones. We've killed one another over less."

Enough for us, I thought to myself, but even with severe rationing, everyone in the sectors would soon die of dehydration. Sounding the alarm to the populace would start a war over what remained, and then, we'd all die anyway.

This must be the true reason for the supply embargo.

I bet the One World ruling class members were behind it. No one in 215 knew their identities or what they looked like, only that they were not likely people of color, were ruthless, and would kill anyone or anything to enlarge their rations. The wealthy populace members would readily accept our demise to their benefit.

Not like I could blame them. Facing death, I'd have done the same. Life is life.

After unscrewing the canteen's top, I reached toward the biodome's fissure to dip it below the surface. Eight stopped my hand and gave me a white device shaped like pliers. "Don't contaminate your collection with your hands," she said. "Use these to limit the exposure."

I did as she instructed. In the sparse light, large pipes tunneling north were visible beneath the surface. The water hadn't run out at all. It was being siphoned. My home was in the southernmost sector. Our neighbors would die first.

FOUR

Eight holstered her Ordnance and positioned herself close to me. "Your mistress is beyond earshot. She can't hear us over the wind gusts. Tell me how we got here and why I'm here, why you're here. I'll try and get us out."

She wanted an explanation. So did I, and nothing I could tell her would likely satiate her desire to know details. When I did not answer fast enough, she continued to talk.

"Start from the beginning. Last night," Eight continued, "I went to the trading post because we agreed to meet. Remember, because you needed water? And then, you don't show."

Angry with myself for freezing up and hesitating, I tried to clarify. "I—"

"Twenty-Three stole radioactivity resistant prototype vegetation seeds, got executed for it, and then, the lockdown started." Eight took the metal canteen I gave her, filled it, and then handed it back. "A fight broke out over the remaining water, and I barely escaped with my life. Did you know about this? You don't seem surprised at all."

I'd caused a great deal of it. A lot of good the seeds did now—we wouldn't get the chance to grow or replicate them. Our future depended on finding a different way to save ourselves and our home. "I have seen it all before."

"Meaning—"

Eight deserved the truth, but I'd never revealed anything about myself to anyone. I'd never had a confidant or a close friend. The facts were harsh and difficult to accept, even for me, and I was the one living through them.

"Nothing. Have we not seen this all before?"

"Not like this." She'd bought my lie. "Your Almunashiy's friend, what's her trick? How'd she get us here, quantum displacement? Technology like that does not exist yet, I don't think, but if it does, we'll have to get the device away from her to escape."

Nazirah and Almunashiy had a prior relationship, and somehow, that knowledge and involvement with my birth

50

gave her naming rights to my abilities, but what should I call hers? "Her name is—"

"Name? She has a forename? Those are forbidden."

I nodded. "Nazirah. Almunashiy knows her. You'll have to ask her about how we got here. She intends to take us to Vagrant City, wherever or whatever that is."

She rubbed her shaved head and said nothing. I knew she would never broach the subject with either of them. To intrusively question elders was a forbidden social practice. We'd find out only if Nazirah wanted us to find out. Otherwise, we would be left to hypothesize.

"Vagrant City is a legend," she said. "Someplace exists ungoverned by One World and the ruling class? Doubtful unless One World runs it. Nobody who set out to find it has ever returned."

This magical place, Vagrant City, intrigued me. A place without direct governance had to mean it possessed resources like decent food, water, and clothing. No droids.

Were these our last days on the planet, I wanted to live like that and not simply exist until I didn't.

"Do you trust Nazirah?"

I did not know who I trusted anymore, but risking death to cross the borders and then bringing us to the middle of nowhere to kill us made no sense. "Almunashiy does not, but our other option is to go home and be shot or starve to death."

Soon, she and Almunashiy appeared, and we walked following their lead. With what we collected and stored, we'd be able to subsist for a day or so even if our collective thirst defied reason. At our current pace, according to the distance marker, we'd be halfway to 610's southern border by tomorrow afternoon.

"Where is Vagrant City? And who are you?"

Nazirah smiled at Eight's question and spat out a black particle clump the size of a small rock. "I am a friend."

"Friend of whom? Her Almunashiy?"

"To you all," she said with a waving gesture. "I will not harm you. Now, what is the farthest north you have been, Eight?"

"I've never left Sector 215's borders. Neither has One, I can guarantee you that."

Regardless, she posed the same question to me, and I pretended not to hear her over the western gusts. Nazirah stopped walking and turned toward me. Pointing her left index finger at me, she repeated the question. "How far north have you gone?"

Eight jumped in. "One, you've never left 215, right?" When I didn't move or answer, she took that as an affirmative response. "See?"

Almunashiy cocked her head with expectancy. I must tell the truth. My breath hitched in my chest. "Six-one-zero. Compound inside of the southern gate."

By the way Eight's mask shifted, I could tell her jaw had dropped. "What?"

The truth weighed on me, so I released it. "I stole the seeds, not Twenty-Three."

Eight drew her sidearm and aimed at me. Almunashiy pointed her Ordnance at Eight, and Nazirah stepped in to shield me.

"Get out of the way, or I'll shoot you, too," Eight shouted. Her sharp words told me she was serious, but Nazirah did not stop blocking me. She fired five times. While one of the shots traveled over our heads, the remaining four hit Alumnashiy in the face and did not harm her. Eight removed her goggles, I thought, to see the proof with her own eyes. They were stun-level blasts and had done nothing to my mentor.

"What are you?" she asked Almunashiy.

My mentor held out her hand and tenderly spoke. "A friend. Stop this and give it to me."

"He was my friend," she cried, her face flush with anger. "And you lied to me. You let Twenty-Three die for you, for what you did!"

"You wouldn't have understood."

Eight repositioned herself to try and get a clear shot at me. Nazirah moved with her.

"Drop it, Eight," Almunashiy yelled. *"Now!"*

"An innocent person died, and your charge said nothing."Using her thumb, she switched the Ordnance to kill. "Why? Why should she live and not Twenty-Three? No. Not happening. I'll kill all three of you."

There was no short explanation, and I had no time for nerves. "Wait! Nazirah calls this an Omnikhron," I said while opening a portal.

Almunashiy cursed me and holstered her weapon.

"It's a black hole that folds distance. This is how I got in and out of 610. I promise I don't know why the droids killed Twenty-Three."

"Because of you!" Eight screamed at me. "They thought he did the stealing."

Nazirah turned to Almunashiy. "Twenty-Three was in the Cloner's Guild. You permitted him access to the strand I gave you, didn't you?"

Cloner's guild? There is a guild?

"I needed help with the gene sequencing to create her, and he gave me ideas I had not even dreamt of."

"Then it wasn't the seeds at all." Nazirah spit out more black particles. The residue stained her chin like a crooked beard. "Your friend must've talked about the replication process to the wrong person. Perhaps he did not reveal your breakthrough, and that is why he is gone."

Me, in other words.

Eight's voice quavered as she lowered her firearm. "He did a lot for all of us."

Almunashiy had always passed me off as an authorized birth, but in the pit of my stomach, I always knew that was fraudulent. Missing limbs and deformations were common in cloned humans since even the most refined fission process had its flaws. To anyone who asked, she'd told them I'd caught my hand in a piece of machinery as a child, which forced her to amputate it.

I looked down at my prosthetic hand and flexed its fingers. It had been calibrated to simulate a real extremity down to the skin tone and nerve endings, but it wasn't real. Pain or pleasure translated through it the same way. Which begged the question: how real was I with no parentage or familial history? To me, the only thing that made living my life of any consequence to anyone were my abilities.

While Nazirah and Almunashiy engaged in a side conversation, the stabbing behind my eyes reminded me I'd left the Omnikhron open above my fist. "Thanks for not shooting me," I said while preparing to close it.

"Wait!"

Eight marveled at the whirling blue portal and its intricacies and whispered to herself. Before I could stop her, she touched the Omnikhron's edge, which I had never done myself. Her fingers passed through to the other side and vanished. She yanked her hand back and regained them. White smoke trails emanated from her gloved fingers. "My hand is numb."

"It's the temperature change," I explained. "The area between wormholes, I call it the Narrow Space, is similar to that of an outer space void. No heat. No oxygen."

"How did you gain this ability?"

I shut the Omnikhron. "I don't know."

Eight's eyes narrowed. "You manipulate the portal's light and environmental radiation, retain your own structural mass—"

"Eight..."

"—control the gravitational pull, escape the event horizon, manipulate the exotic particles surrounding your person, jump across space—and you have no idea how you do this?"

My brow furrowed. Everything Eight said was confusing. It was the same as when Almunashiy talked about my powers; I understood some of Eight's words but not what they meant.

56

Eight stared at me. "The gravitational pull in a black hole alone should crush you, not to mention the radiation. You must control it on a subconscious level, you must! What about time? Can you cross timelines, too?"

Pretending to misunderstand, I asked her to repeat herself. She explained, using more terms I could not understand, that space and time should be under my control in exiting a wormhole. "No," I told her truthfully.

"Makes sense you could manipulate both. You probably just don't know how."

I didn't *want* to create more chaos. What good would it do to fix one mistake and create a host of others? If anything, I'd want to erase the errors I'd already made.

My mentor positioned herself next to me and indicated Nazirah and Eight should do the same. We stood in a small circle. "Take us midway to 610," she said while showing me a digital map. "Here's the klick marker. Nazirah will take over from there."

The trade routes had digital markers every half kilometer. Once I located the correct marker, I previewed its actual location, the terrain, and potential environmental dangers. Seeing no issues, I pictured the marker in my mind and gave out instructions. "Hold hands," I said. "Empty your lungs as much as possible, and quickly follow me through to the other side."

57

I cast the Omnikhron and led the others through—first Almunashiy, then Nazirah and Eight. Aside from my aching brain, I passed through to the other side with no incident. Nazirah took a moment to rub her arms and shake off the Narrow Space's chill. Of the four of us, she was dressed the lightest and had the most exposed skin. Had she spent a couple of seconds longer inside, she might have experienced severe frostbite.

After she drank a full canteen of water, Nazirah said, "Focus will offset the nausea brought on by teleportation or molecular displacement."

"I swear I won't vomit this time," Eight said.

I could only hope as much. Turning my concentration inside, I closed my eyes, held my breath, and waited for the shift in orientation. Once I was certain my feet were on different terrain, I looked around. A gaseous, foul-smelling, green cloud puffed in front of us. The purplish-red skies swirled without rhythm. Was this happening to anyone else? I stumbled backward and moved my mouth to say something, but I don't think I did beyond an unintelligible gurgle. Almunashiy's firm grip held my arms, but the strength in my knees gave, and my vision went dark.

I came to lying flat on my back beneath the sound of rushing wind and heavy, flapping material. Strange, unfamiliar fingers scrambled across my body. Where was Almunashiy or Eight? Would no one defend me from this raider having his way? My entire left side was numb, my muscles burned, and he wanted sex? Men really were the worst, and I was too weak to fight anyone.

A sharp prick nicked the bend in my left arm. Soon, the little world I saw spun and blurred again. Nothing could stop what was about to happen to me.

I squeezed both my fists, felt an electric shock up my arms, and fainted.

Things were black except for the thin daggers of what had to be artificial light shining on my right side. I lay on a makeshift pallet of musky blankets and pillows. Everything was audible, but the clinking metal and rustling made no sense without orientation. Though my eyes stung, I quickly scanned the room. The compound was reinforced fabric, odd-shaped, longer than wide, and decorated with different objects, *alien* objects. Almunashiy and Eight squatted in the top right corner of the room. Seated to their right, my left, was Nazirah.

"Welcome back, bint," she said. With a one-handed push, she staggered to her feet. "You're in Vagrant City." She limped to my side.

The rumors were true, then, about the rebels living in the wilderness. These people scratched and clawed an existence together *better than us?* Eight was right. It had sounded like a legend or myth before now.

Nazirah crouched beside me and reached for my left arm. I flinched. "Easy," she purred. She detached the medicine disk. "Just a little something to steady your equilibrium. How are you feeling?"

Against my better judgment, I allowed her to work. Skepticism was second nature. Almunashiy and I had an unwritten rule to trust one another. And, although I did not intimately know her, Eight had risked her life to save mine, albeit in a different timeline, but she'd earned the benefit of my doubt. These women held wisdom and the perspective age and experience bring. I did not. I was not trustworthy for that reason.

In this instance, I dropped my guard a little. "Ribs are sore. I have a headache."

"Your Almunashiy carried you here on her shoulders." She wagged her bony index finger at my face. "Your body is overwhelmed. The broken capillaries in your eyes could be nothing, elevated blood pressure, or a mild stroke. We don't have the equipment here to tell for sure."

High blood pressure was enough of a problem. A stroke meant slurred words, paralysis, and confusion. I had none of those symptoms besides general disorientation. Based on my timepiece, I had slept for more than a day. Sweat beaded at the base of my neck and armpits. I fought through the medicinal haze to sit up. Crude, circular tattoos were inked on the palm of Nazirah's outstretched hand. I eyed its contents—a brown bowl and a slender silver tool, wide and rounded at the end. "This," she said, "is called a spoon. Dip it into the broth—"

"Broth?"

"The liquid is called broth. Lift it to your lips and drink it."

Hesitating seemed the judicious thing to do, but Almunashiy would not allow me to be poisoned. Its temperature was deceptively cool, so I voraciously sipped. The brackish flavor was like our rationed water when the purification process didn't properly finish, but it was tasty.

Soon, the liquid was gone, and the front of my top was damp from when I'd messed up and missed my mouth. "What is this made from?" I asked.

Almunashiy refilled my bowl from a flask. "Water and animal bones. They harvest their own living here."

"How?" I slurped. "Animals are extinct, and it's too far away to barter or steal from any sector, isn't it?"

No answer from anyone. A secret perhaps. They did not know either.

"Come, my sister and daughters," she said. Stretch your legs, and let's all talk." Nazirah rose from her seat. "It's a beautiful afternoon."

I'd call the weather many things—turbulent, unpredictable, violent, nasty—but not beautiful. I'd never seen anything to describe that way. Certainly not me or this messed-up post-nuclear island.

I got to my feet. After a day without use, my leg muscles had to be urged into cooperation. Wouldn't we need armor to protect our bodies against the elements? Nobody stopped to dress heavier than the thin gray garments I wore, and even the mildest days in 215 would shred unprotected skin. My eyes met Eight's. She was skeptical as well.

"Here." One by one, Nazirah pressed a blackened pair of goggles into our chests. "These are all you'll need."

After I put them on, I followed Almunashiy outside. The sky was slate gray and brighter than I'd ever seen. The goggles blocked most of the incessant brightness, and what passed through them forced me to squint. Vagrant City reminded me of home with its small community of a dozen evenly spaced, weird-shaped fabric compounds. But it was a community unguarded by walls or gates. This made no sense. Why did the government leave them alone and no one else?

Almunashiy and Nazirah spoke to one another in hushed, aggressive tones. Eight and I, on opposite ends of them, tried interpreting the conversation. I had no context for most of the scientific-sounding words they used. It was English but sounded like a different language.

"Hey," I mouthed to her behind their backs. "Why are we here? Am I not supposed to be training?"

Eight put her palms up and shrugged.

Over the next half klick, I waited for a moment to interrupt—a dust cloud, firestorm, acid rain, harsh wind, *something*. Once it became obvious they were not going to stop talking for our benefit, I interrupted.

"Nazirah, you said I was needed here. Needed for what? What could you possibly need from me? What am I to be training for?"

The procession stopped. Nazirah gestured toward Almunashiy. "We have a problem."

"A problem?" I repeated. What did I have to do with this?

Nazirah asked, "Is she ready?"

We all looked toward Almunashiy, whose face registered doubt. "We have no choice."

"Your Almunashiy and I have a transactional relationship. She contacts me with requests: armor, munitions, spare parts. I call her when I need her. Face-to-face meetings are for *costly things.* "Nazirah growled. "This time, I came to her."

"Why?" Eight and I said at the same time.

Nazirah continued. "To forestall the end of all we know."

FIVE

~~~❧~~~

I had not noticed, but we had come to a plot of land where the dirt had been freshly burned. I heard a distinct crack upon my next step, and after lifting my boot, I realized I had broken a scorched bone shard—perhaps a toe or a tooth from the fragment's size. Nazirah had brought us to a burial site. When somebody died, our options were limited in Sector 215. With the sparse land available, cremation was our only recourse and, in absence of proper buildings, they were burned in marked-off areas forbidden to anyone but the cremator.

We now stood in one of these places. Nazirah bowed her head in reverence for a moment. We followed suit. She paused longer than I had originally anticipated.

Her hair dangled in front of her face, but her head and shoulders rhythmically spasmed—was she crying? Praying?

"Last Sunday night." Her voice lowered to just above a whisper.

She continued speaking, but her words faded to silence and moving lips. The violent motions told the rest. With her good hand, Nazirah made a fist the same way I did to use my abilities down to the way my thumb pointed outward—and chopped the air in front of her throat.

Had this person, *this murderer,* beheaded these residents?

Was she accusing me of cutting off their heads with my portals?

I wasn't there. I was in Sector 610, the Narrow Space, avoiding my own death, or in this divergent timeline. I surrendered my hands to reinforce my innocence. "It wasn't me," I said in full voice. "I didn't do this."

Nazirah hushed me. "When speaking of this phenomenon," she whispered, the living residents do not openly do so for fear the killer *or killers* may hear and return."

The idea someone could surveil in open air without one knowing made my skin crawl. Considering what Nazirah and I could do, how outlandish was invisibility?

And, even worse, if a pair of them did this in tandem—one listened while the other acted.

The timing of the assassin's appearance was suspect, and I understood why she could have considered me—the disappearances began on Sunday when I started this timeline with entropic duplicates and alternate timelines. I must hold a degree of complicity. Perhaps this person had been imprisoned, and through my actions, I had unknowingly liberated them.

Regret weighed on my soul. With a lump forming in my throat, I whispered, "Had anyone been able to identify the assailants?"

Nazirah said, "No, except the manner in which it slayed. The victims' heads would suddenly disappear with an Omnikhron around the throat and then reappear disembodied from their necks. Nazirah had attempted to save one of them, but before she could teleport away, the person had been decapitated. All she could recall of the assault was a flood of cold air and the thunk of dropping heads, snapped bones, and tearing sinew breaking the silence.

She did not come out and suggest a connection between me and what happened. She did not have to. I did. Speaking of those with unnatural abilities, I wondered aloud why our own people would turn against us. Nobody offered an answer beyond jealousy, and perhaps that's all it was. But slicing off Nazirah's friends' heads seemed more deliberate than randomly malicious.

"Whatever you want me to do, I cannot do," I said.

Nazirah waved her hand and shook her head. "Will you do nothing? We will wither and die from the supply embargo, too, and if we do not, perhaps the person who graciously liberated the heads of my friends from their bodies will return to finish us and you all as well."

Almunashiy's nostrils flared. "Then, you brought us here to die? What do you suggest, old friend?"

"Accompany me, *ukhti*, all of you, to 267, to end it all."

A bold plan to be sure. Journey to the government's capital, and for what? A quicker death? No way we could break the supply blockade alone, and should we be successful, would we survive it?

"Planning on staging a coup d'état?"

Almunashiy's joke did not draw laughter from her friend. "Of a kind," she said.

Nazirah was serious.

"My mistake for not asking exactly what I signed up for by staying," said Eight, "but whatever you said it was, you didn't mention an out-and-out suicide mission."

One World's predecessor, the United States, had been a democratic republic for hundreds of years. Now disassembled and totalitarian, it had absolute written and unwritten laws. The governed were not to approach those who governed unless called upon. By showing up without an invitation, we could be imprisoned, put to death, or both.

And she wanted to try to overthrow *that*? How?

Nazirah gathered us into a tight circle and bound her hair into a ponytail. She moved her lips slowly so that we could follow and mouthed, "We stop the world from becoming this way."

The words stabbed like a hot blade in my heart. Nobody would have a greater responsibility here than me. Only one of the four of us could manipulate time.

This was to be my training.

Back inside Nazirah's tent, we spoke with greater freedom. Eight and I knew some history, but from the way Nazirah and Almunashiy described what the former world must have been like prior to all of our births, it sounded as if they shared similar fantasies or collaborated on making up the same lie. They claimed Earth used to be vastly populated, overpopulated in places, lush with greenery, teeming with livestock, and composed of large water bodies.

I always pictured the people as various shades of brown with most light-skinned, like me, the landscapes a bright, healthy green, and the water crystal blue. I'd never seen animals to know what they looked like, and our historical archives were devoid of illustrations like we would not miss what we did not know about. Of course, I'd heard words like fish, cow, chicken, and turkey, but aside from understanding they once were used for food, they were nonsense to me. Our protein packets were supposed to taste like them.

"But *how* did it happen?" I asked them, "And when? Where?"

"We don't exactly know," Almunashiy admitted. "But One World does—"

"—which is why we must go," Nazirah added. "There are records of the truth. Then, we can reverse it."

"Time-hopping outside of our lifetimes guarantees that we will not encounter our duplicate selves," Almunashiy explained.

Good. Seeing myself die again was not tops on my wish list of things to do. Once we succeeded, we would live in the new reality I'd create.

Eight scratched her chin. "Sure. All we have to do is get into the most secure sector there is…"

"I can get us through to 454, and—"

"—and, Nazirah, you can keep us alive long enough for One to do something she has no clue how to do?"

"We must have faith," she assured her.

"Faith?" She pointed at me in jest. "In *her*?"

The implication in dedicating oneself to such a mission was that some of us might not survive. This did not appear to be sufficient for Eight, who continued debating with Nazirah over the plan's plausibility.

"Whoever heard of such things as quantum mechanics and string theory taking root in reality? And, even more so, a being like One wielding the ability to control them?" Eight shook her head.

"I will take you back," Nazirah said.

Eight waved her off. "No thanks. I'll make my own, non-spooky, way."

She said it as if she did not expect to see me ever again, which, regardless of my success or failure at what I did next, she would not. It was not appropriate to embrace Eight though a part of me hungered for a touch. We would not exchange any pleasantries. I simply nodded to her and said, "Goodbye."

Eight packed up her things and departed from the tent. I wondered if she'd survive wherever she went, as 215's borders might be guarded, but it was no longer my problem. Once the plan worked, everyone I knew besides

Almunashiy and Nazirah would not be alive yet. *Twenty-Three*. Twenty-Three would have a chance at another, extremely different existence.

Or not.

Would the circumstances of their creation change enough to prevent their existence? And if it did not, it was up to us to eliminate those responsible?

Until sundown, the remaining vagrants—there were just a handful besides Nazirah left—defended the city against One World invasion and the assassin who had nearly cleared the city. Then, at the nightly supper gathering, where the residents ate and "held court," the five of us would hash out our next steps.

I prodded Nazirah about the kind of defense the residents waged that kept droids or drones from razing the place. Their family, the small community, guarded itself. Her answer unnerved me and made me think about the meaning of family. The word had a Latin root, *famulus,* which meant servant. In English, the expression referred to blood relations or close relationships. Eight, my one friend, was gone, and my ancestry and parentage were mysteries. I never asked about them. In a way, I guess, I feared hearing the truth—that Almunashiy was the cloner who mixed my genetic material, and she never cared for me beyond that.

Therefore, I must have no servant, no family.

■・● ●・■

Before we left the gravesite, I asked our benefactor a slew of questions about everything. All she did was grin and educate me about what Almunashiy had taught me or I already knew—our identification numbers were One World ownership labels. We belonged to it like occasionally fed, domesticated pets.

Nazirah tried reassuring me. "I know the way into 454," she said. "What we do works the same in that, if we can picture it in our minds, our powers will usher us there."

"But, over time, the mind loses its grasp on details. Was not relying solely on a mental picture inherently dangerous? Suppose construction—or destruction—had taken place? We could teleport into a fleet of droids or worse...*a wall*."

She nodded and tapped the smartwatch on her wrist. A rotating hologram of an exterior substation adjacent to the city emerged. "Indeed! Which is why I have this."

"And how did you come across a hologram of this military installation?" Almunashiy asked.

"Wouldn't you like to know," she said, winking at us. The social cue was unfamiliar to me. "But, you two will need to blend in. Your identification numbers must be removed along with any mark of life from 215."

73

Though we were lower class, we could not appear so. While my stomach was no longer distended, if I inhaled, my ribs poked through my sides. My eye whites were yellowed with jaundice, Almunashiy's, too. Nobody who met us in passing would mistake us for being above destitute. Sure, they could erase our identification label. Everything else was a different story. And, what about my severed hand? The picture I had always had of those better off than we were was that they were perfect.

Without another word, Nazirah happily hobbled away to the tent's far side and returned with an ancient-looking tool with a short, thick needle aflame at its center. "When you're ready," she said.

I gritted my teeth at the thought—a half-inch flame melting my flesh and whiffing the scent of my own burning skin. Stripping away a manufactured identity would not be entirely painless or without consequence.

And, who was I without the numbers?

Almunashiy sat next to Nazirah and turned to face her. Nazirah adjusted the triangular prongs on the machine until they fit the top of her head, chin, and above her cheeks. The needle rotated to Almunashiy's right temple and ignited a pink laser over her tattooed numbers. White smoke trails emanated from her skin, and I refused to inhale through my nose or concentrate on the hissing sound. All Almunashiy did was clench her jaw and hiss, and her eyes watered a little.

Seconds later, the procedure was over. It did not seem as bad as I had first anticipated. Nazirah handed Almunashiy an adhesive bandage which she placed on the area. "What do I call you?" I asked her. "Are you still my Almunashiy?"

She smiled. "I will always be your Almunashiy."

"But not 5-22-5," Nazirah interjected. "You will take on new identities."

After watching the procedure, I had little qualms about it for myself. I indicated a desire to be next, and Nazirah obliged me. Other than being painful, I was unsure what the experience would be like for me. The laser moved efficiently across my temple and erased the numbers. At its conclusion, I received a larger bandage. Its cool pad soothed my irritated skin. In the eyes of the government, I was no longer 1-13-9-18-1-8.

Inwardly, I felt the same.

The walk to the central gathering was considerably shorter than the one we'd taken earlier in the day to the mass gravesite. They'd erected a circle of twelve weighty stones there and, at its center, angry pillars of raging orange and yellow wildfire. The flames' height and bright hues reminded me of the nights we constructed fires for warmth. My heart ached while remembering my home.

I'd taken my first steps inside its chambers. I wanted, more than anything, to head south to the Hub and everything familiar I'd grown up with. All that waited for us, all that remained, was *death*, and I understood that concept well enough. Or, at least, I thought I did.

The yearnings were strong thanks to the promise of sustenance coming from the fire circle. A stranger tended to the flattened tops of the stones. Another served themselves food. Real food. Not packaged rations but actual vegetables and meat. I'd only ever read descriptions or seen holographic pictures of these things living and was hesitant to try them dead and cooked. I had legs, arms, thighs, and breasts. Using my teeth to pull seasoned and roasted muscle tissue from bones sounded barbaric.

"You always eat like this?" I asked Nazirah. "Together at the same time each night?"

Her response dripped with sadness. "Not anymore."

Almunashiy clutched my right shoulder and pointed her eyes to the stone at nine o'clock. "Vegetables. And try the fish, but be warned, its smell may overwhelm you."

Too late. I swallowed air to ease the queasiness and breathed from my mouth. That helped. Nazirah, flanked by me, Almunashiy, and the two strangers shared a seating area. There was a dish like the broth Nazirah had served me earlier in the day. This version had more cut-up greens, pulses, and a kind of square-shaped yellow protein floating in it that didn't look like animal meat. Nazirah called it a strange word that made me reluctant to explore.

I stuck to the soup and fish with vegetables and tried not to concentrate on the taste. None of it had a soft, chewy consistency like the protein rations I was used to eating. I eyed Nazirah and copied her movements only slower. Once I peeled off the scaly gray skin and stripped away the thin, white bones that thankfully looked nothing like a human's, the meat was soft, flaky, white, and not at all disgusting.

Nobody spoke while we ate. Once the flames died down, the living residents were visible. When I tried sizing them up, they looked away from me and put hoods over their faces. Their need for privacy confused me. Mid-chew, Almunashiy called my name and motioned for me to let it pass. While the vagrants had a right to privacy, I did not understand it, especially if we were to protect one another and work together.

Following the meal, the inside of my mouth was extraordinarily dry. Thirst overwhelmed me. My canteens were back in Nazirah's tent, which was a fair distance away. The vagrants crowded around a receptacle that tunneled into the ground. Its copper lip curved into a receptacle that contained a shallow pool of what I assumed was water. In the darkness and from a distance, it was dark and reflective.

At the same time from opposite sides, the vagrants dipped cups into the pool. Then, bowing their heads, each paused for a moment and then drank. Their actions were quiet, reverential, and contemplative. Almost religious. I'd studied all major faiths. Should I have chosen to follow one, Almunashiy, despite her personal thoughts of religion being pointless, said she'd support me. This ceremony reminded me of the Judeo-Christian tradition of Holy Communion, but unlike Catholics, they did not share the same cup.

What did they think prior to swallowing? Perhaps I should think the same thing.

"This well is more than fourteen hundred feet deep," Nazirah whispered over my shoulder. Before my lips parted to ask, she added, "Our water isn't purified by science like your reservoir."

Then how?

Nazirah took her turn. Afterward, she turned to me. Her brown eyes sparkled and danced. "Do not worry, it's potable. Drink deep, and do not be afraid of what you see or experience. Afterward, we will talk about your training tomorrow."

It was my and Almunashiy's turn. We exchanged a glance across the sacred water. We'd pay reverence to that which we did not understand together like we'd done most things. I stared into the reflective surface and observed my bandaged head. I reached to touch it, thought twice about it, and reset my hand on the cupholder.

Like we'd seen the others do, we dropped the cups and holders beneath the surface and drew the collected water. When mine emerged, its polished, smooth surface was unnaturally cool to the touch. Almunashiy and I raised them, as if we toasted one another, and we spent a moment in contemplation. I quieted myself. All other sounds faded away. My heart thrummed. I anticipated the water's taste and how it compared to the low-quality, barely filtered stuff we subsisted on.

I put the cup's rim to my lips and sipped. The cold, clean liquid chilled my tongue and teeth on the way down. When I thought it had run out, there was more. I closed my eyes and guzzled the rest, savoring every swallow. The urge for more hit my belly, and the cup obliged. Surely, I had imagined, exaggerated, or hallucinated how long I'd been standing at the well's mouth. I felt more energetic and alive than ever before!

I opened my eyes and immediately noticed everyone's focus on me. Or, more specifically, my right hand and left wrist, which were bathed in bright blue light.

SIX

While the others noticed the illumination, I experienced something entirely different.

Usually, the energy swell throughout my body was unpleasant but bearable. This was entirely different...*agonizing*. I dropped to the ground and screamed until my lungs felt aflame. Firm hands tugged at my elbows, and my legs skidded across the earthen floor as they dragged me from the well, careful to avoid my sparking hands.

Had the drink stretched and grown my power levels beyond my limited degree of control? Something in me had changed.

I spit out the saliva flooding my mouth and blinked.

I woke up to almost complete darkness, remembering only a brief flash of vomiting onto the ground.

A figure stood at my feet. Lying down flat on a pallet altered my perception of their height. From here, they might as well have been seven feet tall. Their black shoulders rose and fell every few seconds. I had almost curled my right hand into a fist when a sole with the weight of a human behind it smashed my fingers and pressed my palm to the ground.

My heart leaped.

Screams rumbled from my throat. But nothing came out. My head was inside the Narrow Space. The rest of my body remained in Nazirah's tent.

This was it. I'd been found, and now, I would die.

One breath would end me.

I closed off my scream, held what little breath I had left, and waited for the Omnikhron to close and sever my head from my body. The portal tightened, and while I attempted to assume control of the thing, it would not obey me.

Soon, it would slice my neck.

I waited.

Death had never been shy in his desire to have me, but now, he hesitated. The Omnikhron paused and did not close, I assumed, a fraction larger than the circumference of my neck. I guessed because I could not look. Moving my head at all would submit my neck to the portal's light. My head throbbed, and the moisture in my eyes was hotter than it had ever been. Tired of fighting the urge to breathe, I closed my eyes and, on the count of three, I would open my mouth, inhale a breath, and let Death have his way.

I rushed through the count and breathed. By the time I did, the Omnikhron had disappeared, the person who cast it was gone, and my body was intact. I gasped and coughed, thirsty for air. While my fingers smarted from the sudden pressure and release, and I had no idea what a broken bone felt like, they did not appear to be anything but perhaps bruised.

The worst injury was not mine. Almunashiy crouched next to Nazirah, who rocked back and forth on her knees, shaking and moaning. The sound was awful, a croaking weeping unlike anything I had ever heard. I stumbled around searching for a means of lighting up the tent, and when I was not able to find anything, I used the mechanism on my smartwatch for illumination.

Almunashiy held up her hand to shield her eyes. I turned off the light, but before I did, I saw what was amiss. Nazirah freely bled from both sides of the nose bridge and the front of her neck. Her eyes had been gouged out, and something had gashed her throat. The only explanation was she had seen the assailant, but her injuries were so severe we might never know any details.

When the vagrants arrived, Almunashiy maneuvered to my side and said I should not watch what was to happen next. One of them, the one with the limp favoring their left side, gathered items in the tent to tend to Nazirah.

Together, we left the tent. By the time we reached a decent distance, I heard the echoes of Nazirah's agony.

"They must be cauterizing the wounds," Almunashiy said.

I knew prosthetics were advanced enough to where they could attach to and replicate organ functions, but by the grave appearance on her face, these were not options for Nazirah. It was all I could do to keep myself from hyperventilating.

"What did you see?" she asked me.

He was tall, I remembered, or short. There was no way for me to accurately recall. As I tried, the body proportions shifted in my memory. He was at my feet, so it was impossible to get an accurate measure. My words came out clear in my head but as blubbering nonsense when I said them aloud.

He was fat. Or skinny. *Imposing. Black.*

I sank to the ground and flashed back to the moment when my life almost ended. Covering my face made the images clearer and more frightening. I shook my head. Beyond those minimal descriptors, I could not come up with much. Were this the same person who slaughtered the vagrants and almost killed me, how could we defend against them?

But, then, why take Nazirah's eyes and voice and let her live?

Why threaten my life and not extinguish it?

Why us and not the others?

We stayed away from the tent for a long time. My muscles were so rigid it hurt to move. Though I wore a smartwatch, I was not in the regular habit of checking it. When I did, it was well past dusk on the Doomsday Clock.

Eventually, I stood. My legs, sore from unuse, slightly burned as I urged them forward. Almunashiy led, but the return seemed far longer than the approach. After a while, Nazirah's tent came into sight. The atmosphere was quiet save for the gentle whistling breeze. Nazirah no longer screamed. I wondered if she was dead.

Almunashiy paused at the tent's entrance. "Wait here," she said.

I did not directly disobey her, but I poked my head through the opening before it closed. Nazirah lay still, flat on her back, her chest ever so slightly rising and falling, her eyes and neck wrapped in bloodied white gauze. I gazed at her right wrist. The invader had crushed her smartwatch. They had known that without it I could not go back and save her. We would need her firsthand account to give us an idea of what we were dealing with.

The situation stole my breath. There would be no venturing through the timeline to prevent this wretched reality in which we lived. We would certainly die of starvation now, of thirst, or by the hand of this anonymous assassin. A matter of time in any case.

Four long days had passed. I counted the twelve meals. It was the one time in my life I had eaten three times a day and was consistently full. My system had adjusted to the dietary changes though the acclimations were hardly convenient. I needed looser clothing, and some new food I had eaten was irritating my scalp. My hair had always grown quickly, and since I had no reason to shave, it had passed nearly a half inch. Almunashiy's, too, had thickened enough for her to spend a short time fashioning it.

On those days, Nazirah could not or would not speak. Each day, one of the vagrants—I'd heard Almunashiy call him Zattu—tended to her wounds to prevent infection.

On the second day, Almunashiy allowed me to watch the process once with the stipulation that I not speak. After readying the instruments and concocting a series of strong-smelling salves, Zattu unwrapped the cloth surrounding Nazirah's head. Tossing it aside, he dabbed a clean one into the first bowl and circled the area around the eye sockets. Nazirah barely moved. The cloth's color changed from a soft gray to a dark reddish brown where he had used it.

"Breathe," Zattu reminded her. "Just breathe." Then, he paused before treating the sockets themselves.

Nazirah's voice, or what remained of it, screeched, and her upper body went into spasms until Zattu finished the job. My pulse raced, and I became unbearably dizzy. I resolved not to watch it again.

This morning, the fifth day, following a breakfast of leftover cooked fish and a boiled white grain I could not remember the name of, the other vagrant approached us away from Nazirah's tent.

"Will she speak to us today, Seraphina?" Almunashiy asked.

I casually mentioned the training she'd promised me had yet to begin. Seraphina, a light-skinned woman with thick waist-long braids, motioned for us to follow her. We walked for minutes past the settlement into an open area. There, she closed the fingers of her right hand over her smartwatch and opened her palm. What appeared was a holographic map of an underground room with a number of rehabilitation apartments and biometric chambers.

"We are standing above *this.*" Seraphina pointed to it, and the area throbbed red. She looked at me. "Take us here, please. Now."

I did as she asked and led them to the place. The white room was frigid enough to raise bumps on my skin despite my clothing covering my entire body. "We are running out of time," Seraphina said. "You cannot wait for Nazirah's recovery any longer. You must move."

"But my training," I said. "How can I move to do something I have no idea how to accomplish?"

"Will she speak?" Almunashiy insisted on an answer.

"No," Seraphina said. "Her vocal cords are severed and her larynx destroyed. She will never audibly speak again. Nevertheless, you must go forward. We are running out of time, and you are our only hope."

The news struck me in the chest. Almunashiy, too, seemed affected. Hope for what? How could we succeed without our guide? I wanted to know. Almunashiy's eyes warned me not to ask. Crossing my arms, I tried to soften the scowl on my face to no apparent avail.

Seraphina pointed us forward. Judging by the curved striation on the far wall, we could only go in that direction. Side by side, the three of us approached the first of the rehabilitation apartments. Nazirah was inside. According to the illuminated display, she was alive with a weakened pulse and had been there for hours. She was in a medicinal coma so the apartment's mechanisms might heal her. They'd have to. We were stranded in this place with a lone directive—to enter 267—but without her, we had no idea how.

Seraphina unlatched two of the biometric chambers. These were for us. "Select your options here," she said while bringing up the machine's display. "Choose carefully."

I imagined the biometric machine would alter everything about us. Could the 3D printer replicate authentic-looking and -feeling hair? According to the holographic option menu, yes, it was capable of reproducing hair down to the DNA with length, thickness, texture, and vibrant color options. The result would knit with our hair fibers—*become actual hair.*

At home, having hair anywhere above the armpits was impractical without a steady water supply. Which was another story. The chamber would laser any other hair off our bodies. I wondered what my skin would feel like without the gentle hairs coating my arms and the spiked carpeting under my arms, on my legs, and in my private area.

I could also lighten my skin tone. People in 457 or 267 would not be brown like me. I pictured them whiter than anything I had ever seen, tall, with full golden hair, brightly colored eyes, and healthy, full bodies. Of course, my studies included pictures of people from different ethnicities, but the mid-twenty-first century interest in eugenics had led to a largely homogenous population. Based on that, I decided against the chemical peel. While I had been ridiculed one way or another for being a mongrel, a part of me could not give up that part of who I was.

Also on the list of options were new identities with matching forenames. Only three available ones remained—Amirah, Eve, and Harlow. I took a liking to Amirah and Eve, which meant source of life. Nothing about my existence spoke to the birthplace of anything, so I chose to be Amirah. Almunashiy could choose from the others. I selected a hair texture to match my natural kinky waves and shoulder length so I wouldn't have to deal with management much.

"You will be retrained and reeducated," Seraphina said. "Programmed into your capsules are books we've taken from One World and digitized into memory uploads." She opened her palm that contained two golden pills larger than I thought I could swallow. "Chew these," she said to my relief.

I could not help asking. "What are they?"

"An advanced nootropic," she said. "Chewable in case water is at a premium. Without it, your brain will not process or keep the information you implant. To assimilate into One World's culture, you will need to know more modern history and traditions. I also wouldn't skip the fighting techniques for self-defense. Again, choose wisely."

Direct implants into the limbic system carried a great degree of risk. My brain could only hold so much, which was why Almunashiy forbade it and made me read and memorize everything. That way, I chose what to prioritize to remember.

Under the circumstances, though, we did not have that kind of time. I would have to be judicious and a bit lucky to choose the right uploads. I chose world history, of course, methods of preparing nouveau cuisine—which, I suspected, I'd never use—Jeet Kune Do, boxing methods, parkour, and capoeira. Next, I added first aid techniques, global languages, world religions, a collection of languages, and financial literacy. Last, I chose quantum physics, quantum mechanics, and string theory.

Training for my special abilities would not be included as apparently none of my predecessors were powered or had the opportunity, sensibility, or compassion to leave instructions.

While Almunashiy considered her options, Seraphina took my left wrist, detached my prosthetic in one quick motion and crushed its metal as if it were made of paper. She had strength commensurate to or exceeding Almunashiy's! The metal pins and fixtures popped, and debris rattled against the floor. "The chamber will make a new hand for you," she said.

I had no choice but to believe her. Following a lengthy healing cycle for my scalp, regrown hand, falsified fingerprints, and coded retinas, I'd emerge a new person. I would be Amirah, whoever she was, and how would someone accept me for being past my actual age?

I hesitated before lying down. This was the end of me as I knew me to be. Seraphina closed the chamber and keyed the anesthetic sequence. Gas streams hissed through small openings in the lid near my face, and I panicked. Being confined, trapped in this transparent grave, sapped my breath. I coughed and slapped the reinforced panels. From the wrinkle in Seraphina's brow, there was cause for concern—not enough, however, for her to halt the process. She folded her arms with a loaded Ordnance in her right hand to protect us while we were under.

This put me at ease. I inhaled and allowed my limbs to relax. The urge to close my eyes in submission overwhelmed me. I blinked until lifting my eyelids cost too much energy, and a thick black curtain fell across my consciousness.

All I remembered about my dreams was they were wild conglomerations of thoughts, floating words, events, and mixed emotions.

I awoke with a dry mouth, rested and confused, with no concept of how much time had passed since I had entered the infirmary. What was my new name again or my old one, for that matter? They lingered at the front of my memory, and for a minute, I struggled and scratched my itching scalp. Numbers.

One, I reminded myself.

Not that anymore. I'd adopted a different one to assimilate in the city.

Amirah Mostafa.

The powerful anesthetic worked throughout the entire augmentation process. Though the sensations in my eyes and fingertips were like burning fire, I didn't remember the process at all. Still, I felt like 1-13-9-18-1-8, but I could no longer identify as such.

Condensation lined the casket's transparent insides, and it blurred the outside world. Had Seraphina remained standing guard? She could not have left without me. In all truth, it no longer mattered. What was done had irrevocably been done. My fingerprints and parts of my DNA and retinas were no longer mine. I grieved One. Who was this Amirah? I did not know her. I must discover exactly who I'd become.

When the chamber opened, I sat up and slung my legs over the side. However long I'd been under, my muscles knew the difference. I slid from the elevated platform to the floor and wobbled from the weight shift. Seraphina caught me by the arms and led me to a seat. "Easy," she warned as I lowered myself onto a soft white couch. Next to it was the Ordnance she'd wielded prior to my coma. "How do you feel, Amirah?"

I reached to scratch my scalp. Instead of a bald head, I had plugs of thick, kinky hair! And a new hand. I rotated my wrist. A clear, slimy substance covered my new fingers. When I pulled at the gelatin, it came off all at once. I placed it on the chamber door and looked down at my new limb. All that remained of my disfigurement was a line where my stump used to be. The hand even matched my skin tone.

"Itchy. Why are your lips painted red, Almunashiy?" I cleared my throat. "And why does my voice sound like this?"

My mentor approached. Hair was neatly braided down her back, her eyebrows were no longer bushy but geometrically shaped, and the hair in her nose was no longer visible. She caught me staring at her visage and wiped the lip substance off with the back of her hand. "Experimentation," she stuttered. Her accent was like mine. "You must call me Eve now. Eve Adebisi. Cloning is illegal, and we do not engage in such practices."

Seraphina explained that our new identities were of African descent. This worked for our origin stories. The droids could not question it as the African continent and its almost two billion people had been obliterated long ago.

SEVEN

A glance at my smartwatch revealed I'd need to recalibrate. Its settings relied on the ability to read and calculate atmospheric changes, which were warped below the surface. While I considered how long we must have been comatose, Almunashiy—or Eve Adebisi as I must now call her—revealed the running clock in our chambers. *Five thousand, seven hundred, and fifty-seven minutes.* If my math was correct—it normally was—we were inside them a few minutes short of four days. I reset my timekeeper. *November 28, 2084, 02:00 a.m.*

We took another nootropic. Outside of the chamber, Eve and I would need to chew two a day twelve hours apart to retain the reprogramming. Following today, both of us would only have a six-day supply.

Without them, we would revert to our former, limited selves. The prospect of losing part of my now opened mind in less than a week was a different kind of Doomsday Clock.

My thoughts drifted to Nazirah, whose injuries were far more extensive than ours. Each time I wanted to sneak away to check on her, Seraphina redirected my attention to the task at hand—arming ourselves. The nootropics were hidden in the inside panel of a black synthetic cloth belt she handed us. Eve and I strapped them to our waists.

A boom sounded far above us. Though I hated my new voice, I asked, "What was that?"

They ignored me, which I took to mean do not ask or you do not want to know. This was the way I had been treated most of my life when there were things Almunashiy did not care to explain. I satisfied my curiosity through studies, and when that did not work, I would ask Twenty-Three if it involved males or cloning and Eight for everything else.

Eight. I hoped she made it back to 215, but I imagined she had starved to death or been executed by droids.

And if droids were aboveground and found Zattu, perhaps they had found us.

The white wall behind us rotated, revealing trays of Ordnance and rows of blades. One serrated knife with particularly sharp teeth caught my eye. I went to take it, and Seraphina stopped me. "Munitions are not permitted by civilians in 454 or 267."

A munitions center that disallows munitions? "How are we supposed to defend ourselves?" My new accent would take getting used to.

"Your abilities," she said. Serafina gave us each six magnetized metal balls. "Smoke bombs to mask an escape. Throw one at your feet. The diameter is twelve feet."

Attached to our belts, the bombs appeared to be decorative metal studs. She demonstrated how to detonate one and noted that without appropriate ventilation we would asphyxiate ourselves. Once we finished loading the belts with whatever could be carried in a clandestine manner, Seraphina handed me something—a sensor, I presumed—from Nazirah's smartwatch. "You will need this." She warned me about a notch on the right side. "Touch it, and it will shoot a fatal electric blast at anyone it is pointed at, but with your resting bioelectric charge, it will take days to recharge after use."

I did not have the nerve to kill besides the roaches and other bugs that freely roamed our sector. They were a different species beneath me—unreasoning—but another human had the ability to discern right from wrong and, presumably, a soul that I would send elsewhere by extinguishing the life of its container. For me, pointing the smartwatch at someone with the intent to kill meant accepting those terms.

I was reluctant to accept it, but as I would be the one to take us to 454 and then 267, possessing it made sense. The sensations in my regrown hand were natural. I wiggled my fingers as I added the sensor to my smartwatch. The always present electrical pricking in the prosthetic was gone. Amazing! It was like I had never lost a hand.

Seraphina waved us to the white room's far side. Before we obeyed, tremors shook the room and unsettled our balance. In tandem, we looked up. The ceiling had a barely perceptible fissure in it, and white dust fell from the crack. I cursed in a language I'd never consciously used—Arabic, Farsi?

I spoke both of them.

Another tremor, more violent this time.

Arabic. I had cursed in Arabic.

I sneezed, and we retreated into the next available space, an extension of the armory. Nothing in here, aside from the massive black Ordnance the size of my entire body, could dent the things coming for us. And then, what? Going back to the surface, where these things had gathered, might be worse. While I ran full speed to the next apartment, Seraphina stopped and grabbed something I could not see from the silver table in the middle of the room. With her pronounced limp, she proceeded at less than half our speed, so Eve put her arm around Seraphina's waist and carried her forward.

"Here," she said, handing us a circular black disk. "Place this at the base of your neck." She pointed toward the closest wall and moved her hand the way I did when activating my abilities. "Fourteen klicks west."

I did as she instructed, cast an Omnikhron, and held out my left hand. Eve took it and joined me in the Narrow Space. I waited for Seraphina, but she turned her back to me, and Eve pushed my hand down with hers to close the portal. She had accepted whatever fate awaited her outside of my Omnikhron. I had not known her long enough to grieve for her, but without Nazirah and now Seraphina and Zattu, we were totally on our own.

We journeyed to the other side, fourteen klicks from our origin point. It emptied into a pitch-black tunnel, man-made from its smooth appearance. The nerves in my neck tingled. Fluid metal oozed across my clothing, and though I shrieked and slapped at it to hinder its progress, it adhered to my skin and formed all over my body, Eve's, too. Inside the covering for my face was a holographic display. According to the reading, the atmospheric temperature was fifty degrees, my heart rate was 130 beats per minute, I was at risk of hyperventilation, and the air contained moderate concentrations of a gas called methane, which did not sound harmful but might have been. I suspected the masks filtered out its stench.

"Where do we go?" I still had not grown used to my new voice.

"Forward," said Eve.

The bodysuit heated itself throughout, but I could still feel the chill in the air. It also cast a warm purple glow from its surface about three feet in all directions. Staying close to each other increased the lighting's strength. We kept a steady pace and did not speak much. There was nothing to discuss except when to break into 454. Our walking gave me time to process my thoughts regarding the timing. Right now, it was the middle of the night. Even by 215's security protocol, everything would be locked down, including the gates and the borders, and breaching the city now made little sense.

So, we'd walk until further notice. Soon, the man-made portion ended, and we were forced to climb over jagged, rocky embankments and squeeze through spaces where the earth had shifted into tight pockets. After an hour, my legs and feet burned and ached. The heads-up display showed my pace had slowed from sixteen minutes per mile to thirty-five minutes per mile. Eve was barely ahead of me. How long was this tunnel?

Eve stopped. "Time to rest," she said. "Sit at my back. I will stand guard."

I had little strength to argue. I eased to the floor, sat, and stretched my legs. Eve groaned and did the same, setting her weight against my back. Although my entire frame, from my neck down to the bottoms of my soles, was weary from use, I could not drift off to sleep. Our breathing rhythms did not match. The mask's constricting fit over my face did not help, and even with the brightness turned down, the lights on the display shone through my closed eyelids. I needed a way to relax or find a better use of my time than obsessing over it.

"Who am I?" I asked.

"You are Amirah Mostafa. Zimbabwean, of Bantu origin."

I elaborated. "I mean, where did I, One, come from? Originally."

She knew I meant more than if I was a clone. That was obvious. When she hesitated, I encouraged her to start from the beginning.

"The beginning started with my clone birth long before yours. My parents—I considered my creators to be like parents—died in a 215 riot. I don't remember much about them, images, distorted voices. Then, Twenty-Three raised me much in the way I have done for you."

That explained her reaction to my accident and his demise. "The vagrants were born of flesh and blood parents?"

"Many of them, yes. Not Seraphina."

"Then, where did my abilities come from?" I asked her.

She answered, "Twenty-Three educated me in cloning sciences. You were born of that knowledge. Your genome is a mix of a purified strand from the late twentieth century. Together, we had unsuccessfully spliced genetic marker fills for the strand's gaps over the course of decades. You are the lone survivor of our many efforts."

I did not fully understand the deeper scientific explanation, but from what I parsed, the genome responded to fills from Black, Chinese, and Caribbean DNA, which accounted for my appearance. "But why *that* strand?" As soon as the question left my lips, I figured out why: what I could do. "The source—that person could travel through space and time like me?"

Eve nodded. "We believed so, yes."

"Who gave it to you?"

She paused for what seemed like an eternity. "Nazirah, who got it from One World."

A weight formed in my stomach. *I was property of the government*. Ten days ago, I had every intention of living as long as possible with no aspirations of doing anything grand or world altering. Was that still a possibility, I wondered. Did not seem to be. Especially not with a totalitarian regime.

Suddenly, all the moments I had stolen food and barely dodged capture, including the machine that had tagged me and the raiders whose grasp I always escaped, gained texture. Nothing was coincidental about my existence. I was literally born for this purpose, and One World wanted me to accomplish it or another unrelated one. Otherwise, why preserve a DNA strand from a powered person who could manipulate time?

Eve did not speak for a while nor did I. Weariness had seeped into my mind, and I was tired of thinking. The nootropic helped me process the implanted information. There was so much running through my brain at all times. Like the fact that methane was a fuel found below the earth's surface and was flammable, so we had to be careful not to create accidental sparks.

I sighed. Uncertainty was in front of us. A long death trail lay behind us.

"No one remembers the order of the attack," she continued, "except that Africa was decimated first, and here, North America, was second. Asia, Europe, then South America, and the rest. Without electricity and telecommunications, we did everything possible to survive and help one another.

"These sectors are what remain. Amirah, it is not enough to know *when* this happened in order to stop it. You must know *where,* and we will need to find it in 454."

I yawned twice in succession. "How do you know it's there?"

"Nazirah and her friends gave their lives based on this belief." She yawned as well. "You must remember that Nazirah, Zattu, Seraphina, Twenty-Three, none of their deaths—even mine, should it happen—will be consequential when you succeed."

That knowledge did not comfort me. The task still loomed as impossible, and I had not learned how to control moving through space *and* time. "Will you help me?" I asked.

"Always," she responded.

Now that I was armed with a bit of security, my chin dropped to my chest, and my eyelids grew heavier. All of the talking and maybe some of the gas, too, made me drowsy. I gave in and fell asleep.

Why was she telling me all of this?

Why now?

Were we about to die?

I found myself in the Narrow Space surrounded by dozens of rotating Omnikhron leading to who knew where. Confused, I followed the gentle tug in my belly, chose one, and stepped through. Because of the sun's bright glare, I had to focus on the ground. I'd never seen grass, let alone anything naturally the color green besides an occasional bowel movement. I kicked off my boots and planted my bare feet on the surface expecting to feel nothing. After all, I'd never had tactile sensations while dreaming. So many textures to take in...lush, prickly, softness. I wiggled my toes and giggled when the cool blades sprung up between them.

Once my eyes adjusted, I looked around. Metal, glass, and redbrick geometric structures, black macadam streets emblazoned with white and yellow lines, and different colored four-wheeled transports. I'd seen historical holographic recreations of these things in my studies, but they lacked tangibility. The air was clean to breathe. No methane. People of all ethnicities walked around me.

I approached an empty silver transport and marveled at my reflection in its glass. It was my new look, not from when I lived in 215. My facial complexion was clean, and wavy lengths of hair extended from my scalp. I reached into the mass and grabbed a handful. It was weighty and soft-textured, real, mine.

As I smiled and spent a moment enjoying the ancient sites, a mushroom cloud puffed in the distance—a nuclear explosion. My heart thumped, and I froze. Everyone around me and in the distance gazed at the horizon.

We were all going to burn.

Quicker than anyone could respond, a thunderous wave of destruction and black clouds rolled through and flattened the society in front of me. Charred building shells, melted transport debris, collapsed human skeletons, and towering fire pillars were all that remained. When I accounted for myself, my blackened bones lacked muscle and skin.

How was I alive?

My jaw opened. I screamed for help, loud and violent. I heard it myself inside my open skull.

Somebody had to hear me.

Eve? Where is Eve?

I blinked, expecting the world to change back to the tunnel, my normal living nightmare, but it did not. I squeezed my bony fingers into a ball and hoped for an escape. When no salvation arrived, I awoke to the screaming of my old name. Eve was shouting in my face. No longer back-to-back with her, I was standing at the far edge of the tunnel in front of an open Omnikhron. When I realized this, I closed it.

EIGHT

P art of me ached for the beautiful world I had just
seen. Nothing in the present looked anything
like what I had just experienced. For my entire
life, that world was never tangible to me, and now that it
was, I wanted...*needed*...more of it.

However, I could not fathom where or when it was.

Eve grabbed my arms and shook me. "Listen to me.
This is very important. Where did you go?"

Her force rocked my equilibrium. "I-I...don't know!"

"Check your smartwatch." I compared my display to
hers. The stamp was the exact same. So, I had not hopped
timelines. But where had I gone?

Horrified that I defied logic and started a new timeline again, I steadied myself and described what I had seen in detail.

Eve quietly paced while I spoke. With an expressionless mask covering her face, I had no clue as to her reactions until she sighed.

"You didn't start another timeline." She coughed. "You jumped outside of your lifetime. There do not appear to be temporal consequences."

I could not understand what she was saying through the throbbing in my head, so much so, that I asked her to repeat herself twice. The bright, heads-up display in my mask was blinking with red numbers. Thinking the mask might respond to higher brain function, I instructed the mask to retract, but it did not. Fresh air, not the filtered breaths the bodysuit forced me to take, would help me. *"A-Almunashiy,"* I slurred.

A strong grip clutched my right side. My legs were limp, but I dragged them forward the best I could. The dizziness made this nearly impossible. How much longer could we go like this? Not much, it turned out. We collapsed in a heap on the tunnel floor. I closed my left eye and focused hard on the blinking red display on the right. *Heart rate is 160 beats per minute. Sixty breaths per minute. Methane concentration is 75 percent.*

I waved and stated the obvious. "We have to get out. The gas is killing us."

Eve agreed and pointed up before going limp.

Casting an Omnikhron was the easy part, but without an idea of how deep underground we were, we could end up embedded in the earth's crust. My only other option was to execute Nazirah's plan and breach 454. The time was nearly dawn, and perhaps that meant we would not be executed on sight. Still, I felt we should attempt to approach when my protector was conscious. Grabbing Eve by the wrist, I dragged her with me through the Omnikhron, the Narrow Space, and into open air.

We tumbled several feet to the ground. The bodysuit obeyed my commands and withdrew at the face. I gasped and spit into the dirt. The smell and taste in the air was rancid, like something had died and decomposed. There was a good reason—we were feet from 454's waste pit.

The mask reformed, and I scanned the horizon behind us. A pillar of reddish-orange fire and billowing black smoke blazed in the distance. *Vagrant City.* In front of us, at a comparable distance, was the rear garrison of Sector 454. Its walls were impossibly high and gray either made of stone or stained that color from the environmental soot and acid rain. On its west side was a smaller, more vulnerable building—the same construct from Nazirah's hologram map—without visible armaments.

My companion stirred and moaned from pain. She had caught the brunt of the impact as I had landed on top of her body and pressed her right side into the earth. I appreciated the long groan Eve let out since it meant she had regained consciousness, and I did not have to resuscitate her. It also meant I did not have to plot strategy by myself.

"Are you all right?"

Eve rolled to her knees, got to her feet, and looked around. "We must keep moving."

Remembering how Nazirah conjured the holographic map from her timepiece, I did the same. The images matched. I gestured to the smaller building. "There?"

"Do you know what it is?" she asked. Her bodysuit slithered away back into its disk. Underneath, she had on the same clothes from the biometric chamber. She would look suitable to anyone scrutinizing her appearance.

I despised speculation. "Some kind of substation...a subordinate armament station or barracks?"

"Whatever it is, we have a better chance of survival there than going to 454 blind."

I cast an Omnikhron and commanded my suit to retract. My clothes were damp with sweat around the neckline and at the armpits but presentable. "And what do we do when we get there?"

"Improvise."

We arrived at the building's front step. Its biometric scanners immediately identified me as Amirah Mostafa of Zimbabwe and her as Eve Adebisi of Zambia. I panicked, thinking we should take a nootropic, but we were not due another dose for some hours. Our increased knowledge base might help us with this particular challenge. Prior to my reprogramming, I knew little to nothing about Africa, and I could not communicate in foreign languages though I could read Spanish well enough.

I kept my hands clenched in case we needed to make a quick escape. When the metal door folded inward and retracted, I was not prepared for what I saw inside. It was a droid depot, a repair center, tended to by a tan-skinned human man. He wore goggles with darkened lenses, a black jumpsuit with silver tools pocketed in the arms and waist, and a gray mask over his nose and mouth.

He pointed a specialized silver Ordnance in our faces and said nothing. My fingers twitched. Should he open fire, I'd have a split second to send the blasts into the Narrow Space to protect us. In my peripheral vision, Eve appeared relaxed and not all that concerned about our safety. This was where her friend had instructed us to go, and I had hoped Nazirah had known better than to send us into a trap.

111

He broke his stare long enough to pose a question, his weapon's barrel aimed between us. "On the day before the solar flare, you mongrel women come out here like vermin for whatever I can afford you. Did you not pay attention to the message?"

"Of course," Eve said. "But we thought—"

"Instead of avoiding the safehouses, you should go straight to one?" The man holstered his weapon on his right hip, stepped forward, and looked over our shoulders for anyone or anything that might have seen us. "No, you did not think. We're under curfew. But, at least you did so early in the morning. I'll give you that. Come inside before you get caught in the droid sweeps."

Eve and I entered far enough for the door to have enough room to reform. The building was tall, about twice its height in width, and deep. Stationed to our left, right, and hanging above our heads were deactivated droids similar to what I had seen my entire life. They were smaller than I remembered. Centered on a track was a droid facing us, the one, I assumed, he was repairing when we interrupted.

"I don't suppose either of you have eaten. There is oatmeal on the table, utensils in the drawer beneath. Serve yourself. Dishes are in the sink."

I mouthed oatmeal and utensils to Eve, and she waved me off. I –followed her actions and scooped the stuff into a metal bowl, like the soup bowl I had eaten soup out of at Nazirah's, and ate it with a spoon. The texture was soft and mushy, a little bland, but filling. As we ate, our silent host returned to work on the droid's undercarriage. Only when we finished did he speak.

"You are trusting," he said. "Too trusting. I could have just drugged or poisoned you."

Eve shook her head. "And we could be spies sent to assassinate dissidents."

"One World does not bother me, and I do not bother them." He did not hide his disgust for the government. "So, if you are here to kill me, *do it.*"

The man returned to his work while I took account of my body. I did not feel any different. Had he poisoned us? My throat was dry, but we had not drunk anything, and I was hot, but air did not seem to be circulating much here. That accounted for the strong scents of oil, fuel, and perspiration.

"I have not seen you in 454 before," he said in Xhosa.

I speak Xhosa, too!

"You're Africans, but your features do not *look* African. How did you escape the continent?"

A test. How does one have African-looking features? Eve looked to me to respond since I had learned world languages. I thought about what I wanted to say, and when I spoke, it came out as a series of words and clicks of my tongue against the back of my top row of teeth.

"By the grace and mercy of Almighty God," I responded in Xhosa. "My mother here was on holiday when the attack struck."

"And what of your life mate?" he asked her in English. "Her father. Where was he from?"

"Cape Verde," she said without pausing. "We never made our union legal. Before our daughter was born, he died of bone cancer."

Ironic how, in previous times, radiation was used to cure cancer, but in our world, it caused incurable versions of the disease along with mutations and genetic deformities, so the story was believable and would not provoke questions.

Upon hearing that, the repairman's tone softened a bit. "I will see what I can do for you in the way of weapons. My output is closely monitored, and I can only forge weapons from what I overreport. You understand."

He accessed a hidden drawer in his workstation. There were two small firearms that would conceal well underneath our clothes. Before he grabbed them, he casually said, "Our coded message has been repeated on the analog radio channel for a day. You must have received it, so what made you come here against it?"

"Nazirah," I blurted out before I could help myself.

He dropped the firearms and turned away from his workstation to face us. "What did you say?"

I hesitated in repeating the name, but he insisted.

"Nazirah."

"Nazirah is a myth. Vagrant City does not exist." He approached his workstation and shut the drawer with the Ordnance. "Beings with powers capable of saving what is left of the planet living in a city outside of government rule. I've heard the theories, the fables. We all have. One World commissioning superpowered clones...they're all fairy tales. Our hopes are solely in our hands and not those of god beings."

"It *is* true," Eve protested. "We have seen it!"

Her insistence enraged our host. "Lies! You have seen *nothing!*" He turned a dial on his workstation. The droid he had been working on activated and pointed its weapons toward us. "No, Nazirah did not send you, but we will discover who has."

"She did!" I protested. "Vagrant City is being razed as we speak."

"You *were* sent by One World to execute me. I will not die at the hands of two mongrels."

I formed a fist and prepared for us to escape. "We—"

His droid rapidly fired at us, which I blocked with an Omnikhron wide enough to shield me and Eve, and returned the blasts in its direction with another portal. The lasers ricocheted throughout the bunker.

"Enough!" he yelled over the noise. "Stop! You're destroying everything!"

I closed the portals as the firing stopped. The deactivated droid collapsed with a *thunk*, shaking the floor, and some of the machinery in the background sparked electricity. White smoke trails emanated from the wreckage.

"Now, do you believe?" I asked him. "We are not your enemy!"

Eve glanced at me with a mix of disappointment and scorn. He, however, stared at me in awe. This man had forced my hand. I do not know what she expected me to do besides what I had done. Was I supposed to allow us to be gunned down? Our cloaked suits could not have withstood the onslaught. I knew this. So did she.

Nevertheless, we had been discovered. Either we had to rid ourselves of him or his knowledge of my ability.

Mouth agape, he removed his goggles. "I am 9-19-1-9-1-8, or Nine for short. And *you*," Nine said, wagging his finger at me, "you are vigilantes and are no longer legends."

NINE

C learly, we were not who we pretended to be. That much was apparent from my power display. Since Nine did not seem like he would kill us anymore, and Eve agreed to drop our assumed identities, we told him we were originally from Sector 215.

This shocked him. We had no way to prove it beyond giving him information he could no longer verify. Our numbered tattoos were gone, and when he searched his computer for our original identities, we bore a passing resemblance to our former selves.

Our original identities were flagged as deceased in his system. According to Nine, in the past few days, our home had been the site of an anti–One World protest, and droids had bombed it into glowing ash

At least that was what was reported.

Everyone and everything I formerly knew was dead. There was no going back now. My chest ached as I silently remembered them all. There had to be a future beyond this, but despite my lucid dreams, I could not imagine what it could be.

Nine described himself as a step above a slave in 454's social order, thus his identification number in lieu of a proper forename.

Most of what he said rushed past my panicked mind. I understood the basic points. Military personnel regarded him as weak for not having witnessed field action, and those in "the culture"—the clandestine population who outwardly approved of One World's rule but inwardly disagreed—considered him a valuable traitor.

He resumed working while he talked to match his daily output numbers which, according to Nine, would be the only metric One World monitored.

"I don't mind being underestimated. The government has no reason to come after me, and I am not social anyway, so people can think what they want to think about me."

"But these droids have gunned down entire populations—men, women, children. You don't feel complicit?"

Nine chuckled at Eve. "A precision laser blast ends a life in seconds. Starvation, dehydration, radiation sickness...these things take days, weeks, or months. How would you choose to die? Quicker deaths free up resources faster."

"Sounds like the reasoning of a privileged politician," Eve said.

"Perhaps," he replied. "Solid reasoning nonetheless. And after the festival tomorrow, it won't even matter. The planet will be a charred rock decorated by vaporized structures and ash. These are the final hours they will monitor my output. We work until we die, sort of an anti-Epicurean outlook, wouldn't you say?"

I asked the obvious question. "What is going to happen?"

In days, One World monitors predicted that another of these occurrences would happen. The last few times it had done so, coincidentally, it had been around this time of year. He said that, together, the ones in 2029, 2032, 2035, and 2064 wiped out every continent but North America, and the one in 2074 mostly erased what was left besides what we were standing on. Another one would decimate most of what we knew.

"Then, why work on drones *now*?" I asked him. "Why do anything?"

119

Nine stopped his work and looked at me. "Because I need to see the end of what I begin. Tomorrow, I feast until I die."

For the first time, I accepted why Almunashiy had strived to create me and what I could do. "I can stop this, Nine, but we need your help."

"Stop *what?* The festival? One World has been siphoning water and rationed food from all the minor sectors for this precise, hedonistic reason."

His buzzing tool was impossible to speak over, so I waited and thought about what a celebration before the end of civilization as we knew it might include. None of One World's restrictive laws would matter. Foreign substances, crime, untold debauchery, and destruction— the population's worst sides would show their faces.

And we would be present for all of it.

Nine's voice jumped with excitement when he mentioned the festival and all of its indulgences. As far as we could tell, he was a man with no intimate human companionship to speak of. Who would deny him physical satisfaction should he ask, and if he was refused, would he take it anyway? I gave him the benefit of the doubt his character was not that of the raiders I had grown up around. His demeanor was unsteady, vacillating between kindness and antisocial tendencies.

120

When his work took him to a spot behind the droid's left haunch, I yelled out, "The portals I open manipulate space *and* time."

My voice wavered when I said time, and he caught on to it. "So, you can go back in time to 2029 and stop the world from *this?* Why haven't you? What are you waiting for?"

"Because we need *specifics,*" Eve said in my defense while completely ignoring my control issue. "She cannot go back that far without context. She cannot go without knowing what to stop, how to stop it, and where to find it."

Nine sighed with exasperation. "The historical archives in 267 are your best chance to find out. Good luck getting there. I doubt any mongrel alive has set foot in it."

I squared my shoulders. "Then, I will be the first."

"No, no you will not," Nine argued. "Your existence violates the miscegenation laws and, I'm assuming, the clone laws also. It doesn't matter what the biometrics say about your heritage. You won't get into the congressional library on your skin color alone."

One World should be overjoyed I exist. Being a government-sponsored clone must somehow buy me favor with someone.

"She's not going to knock and ask nicely," said Eve. "With everyone attending the festival, I doubt the library will be as heavily guarded."

"We do not have much of a choice," I chimed in.

Nine continued talking while filling the Ordnance holes in the droid's facade with liquid metal. Once settled, the metal warped colors to match its surrounding panels. "When you use your powers, how close can you get to the intended target?"

"Depends. I need to visualize it first."

"And you can take others with you?" he asked.

"Yes," I admitted.

"Interesting. Will a schematic work for your visualization?"

"Yes, yes, I believe so."

"Good. I know someone who works in the capitol building. I will add your identities and biometrics to the sector's census in place of two mongrel women who recently died."

While Nine worked, there was little to busy ourselves with since he had warned us not to touch anything. We leaned against the north wall and rested in short spurts, first me, then Eve. Before long, it was Nine's lunchtime, and he again offered us a portion of his meal—bread, cooked fish, and water. He said a prayer to some being over it and gave us each a handful of food while reserving a commensurate amount for himself. Once he finished his work, the three of us would depart for the encampment where he resided. There, we would meet the residents and the one person who could get us into the library.

"So, how do you do it?" he asked me. "How do you time travel?"

I admitted the truth. "Thus far, I have only done it by accident."

Nine choked on his food. "You have not mastered it?"

Eve explained to him the dangers of branched timelines and the temporal paradoxes possible when two versions of one person exist in the same reality. I added that Nazirah promised training before her maiming rendered it impossible.

While the look on his face said he understood what *could* happen, with the threat of global extinction in less than forty-eight hours, which *would* happen, the consequences did not seem so weighty anymore. Should I not at least try to figure out how to do it? In the moment, though I was afraid, there would not be any time for guesswork.

"Practice is possible," Eve said. "You'll need to journey outside of your lifetime, and I will need to send you with a reductor if you travel within it."

She rattled off a list of scientific-sounding apparatuses I could not hope to comprehend and asked Nine if he possessed any of them in his workshop.

"Some," he said. "What are you trying to decrease to an atomic level?"

She pointed to me. "Any alternate version of her she may encounter and have to eliminate. I can engineer one from memory."

"Why not just kill the extra copy? The atomic residue is still in existence, so technically, though you have reduced it, the matter is still present."

"But the temporal effect is minimal," she argued. "The paradox is not merely in the duality of her existence, but seeing herself could cause a cataclysmic chain reaction."

Nine stifled a laugh. "Could. More cataclysmic than nuclear radiation frying the earth?"

"I have been contemplating that." Eve leaned forward. "What causes the nuclear explosions? History tells us X-class solar flares preceded them, but those are a means, not the end. By themselves, they cause electrical damage, technological failures, but not much else. They are catalyzing a reaction with—"

He held up his hand and dismissed her. "Nobody knows for sure except that it happens," he said between chewing. "Take whatever you need."

After we finished the meal, Nine went back to work, and Eve and I took nootropic pills and rested some more. Mind reading was not one of my abilities, however, I theorized the explosions might not be caused by a thing but a person like us and believed Eve shared the same view. Was it really that outlandish? Eve had supernatural strength. Nazirah could teleport. I could bend space and time by manipulating wormholes. Someone else could manufacture destructive nuclear energy from a singular source point, and the chaos could mimic ground zero of a bomb's impact.

I would have to go back and keep the world from burning.

Eve wandered around the grounds, collected an armful of tools and equipment, and returned to my side. With the bounty between her legs, she disassembled a silver orb with free-hanging white wires from its bottom. I watched as she rewired the thing and connected it to what appeared to be an Ordnance power board.

"Almunashiy," I whispered.

She leaned to her right, my left, and said,. "You must learn to call me Eve."

"Couldn't the source of the explosions be a person?"

"A person." She was interested enough in my hypothesis to stop working. "How did you come to this theory?"

I moved closer to her to maintain privacy. "Vigilantes. The one who attacked Nazirah. He may have attacked Vagrant City because he knew, she and I together, we could stop him."

"Then, why not kill us all and detonate right there and then?"

I shrugged. "Maybe because he must wait for…"

"A solar flare storm," we said in unison.

Then, I remembered he had almost decapitated me with an Omnikhron. Meaning, should I have to go back to defeat a person, I would likely be overmatched.

"Has there ever been a person who wielded more than one ability?"

Nine employed a drill whose whir made us raise our voices over it. "I heard rumors of an unusable genome strand once," she said. "The owner had strength, invulnerability, and flight. I procured a copy of it from Twenty-Three and challenged myself to clone it, but I could not purify the DNA or fill its gaps."

The power to transport myself across space and time was enough. Once Eve completed a working reductor, I would practice crossing time.

Between the two of them working, the sound was overwhelming. I donned my mask and activated the soundproof setting. Without noise to distract me, I was able to quickly fall asleep.

126

I'd always imagined Sectors 610, 454, and 267 as shining, ethereal paradises like the pre-disaster landscape I had seen when I went back in time in the tunnel. The residents there had to have had it better than us. I anticipated seeing evidence of this as Nine closed up his workshop for the evening and led us toward the aperture in the western wall. My heart raced in my chest. Nine said he had set up our identities in the system. Suppose he had not. We would be eliminated on the spot.

Still, we followed him. At the entrance, a round, black probe emerged from above us and scanned our bodies with a red laser. "Welcome, 9-19-1-9-1-8," it said in an automated voice. The doors slid open. Nine quickly stepped forward, and the entrance shut behind him. I inhaled a deep breath and held it.

"Welcome, Amirah Mostafa."

I mimicked Nine's movements when the doors opened and jumped when the metal slammed together. A few seconds later, Eve joined me. It worked!

We followed him down a dirt pathway where the walls beside us were fifty feet high. I noticed the mounted black Ordnance stationed at regular intervals inside rectangular wall depressions. They swiveled, trailing us along our path. My shoulders and arms tensed in anticipation of an assault. As usual, Eve seemed unbothered by this. What horrors had she seen to make her so callous to danger?

Farther down were entrances built into the walls. Our home was not positioned close to any other, so there was no mistaking where we lived. Here, they did not have numbers or markings indicating to whom they belonged. We matched his pace until it slowed, and he drifted to the left. He gestured for us to wait in the passage while he entered alone. A quick glance inside showed a space lit with warm light. I locked eyes with a woman inside, and we stared at one another. Was she his life mate?

I kicked sand back and forth between my boots to pass the time. Eve and I refused to speak. Surely, after today's events, Nine would not abandon us in this place.

"Here." Eve placed a black and silver pieced-together reductor in my right hand. The machine was a fraction of the one I had seen before. "Strap it to your belt. It resembles a communicator. You have three charges. Do not waste them."

I kept her words in mind when Nine welcomed us inside.

TEN

I n 215, we did not welcome guests often. Between Almunashiy's illegal cloning, the theft I committed on a regular basis, and dodging clandestine informants to the government, entertaining was not wise. Therefore, I had little to no idea about how to act in the company of people I did not know with customs I was unfamiliar with. From the tentative way she moved next to me and fidgeted with her hands, Eve, too, was nervous.

We stood side by side inside the doorway. At the room's center was a mud-brown, cushioned piece of furniture with a backing. Nine gestured that we should round it and sit. Reluctantly, we did so. The cushion gave when we sat on it and relieved pressure on my feet and knees. On the clear table in front of us were two cups.

"Welcome," Nine said with a note of grandeur. "Please refresh yourselves. The water is newly drawn."

Water. I did not reach for it until Eve did, and I followed her lead, taking a small sip. The liquid was perhaps the coldest I had ever tasted besides that of the Vagrant City well. Subduing my pleasure, I swallowed the rest before placing the cup down. Then, a slender, pale-white woman with buzzed, auburn hair entered the room, seized the cups, wiped where they had been with a cloth, and retreated to the next chamber.

Nine waved his hand. "You will have to excuse Thirteen," he said. "Droids scan for lifeforms at dusk, and she thinks they will catch and apprehend you here." His companion shot him an annoyed look, but she smiled at us. Or at me. Her steady eye contact with me and the way she licked her lips were confusing. Was she thirsty? She did not take a drink.

"You put us in the system," Eve said. "Where do we reside?"

"I did not assign you a home. In less than two days, there will be nothing left."

"Why not say we lived here?"

He rolled his eyes and hissed at me. "We are not of the social class to officially do so. I don't imagine they will execute us with the end so near, do you?"

I did not know. The threat of death frequently hung over our heads, so much so that the mention of impending doom did not even make my stomach clench with fear anymore.

The room was bare, save for the table, the silver metallic walls, and what we were sitting on. Knowing Nine's background, there had to be some kind of hidden technology behind the shiny interior. Sure enough, one of the panels slid back on Nine's command. The space inside was large enough for Eve and I to stand side by side. White smoke trails and a blast of frigid air expelled into the room. "The core temperature will mask your heat signature long enough for the thirty-second scan to pass," he said. "I will call Two, he's a friend, for the schematics, and together, we will plot your next steps."

We had not been the first people they had hidden.

"Will we have quarters?"

Nine waved three fingers to the back right of the corridor on our left. "There is a storage space large enough for the two of you to lie down in."

"I would like to see," she said. "You may stay here."

Fine by me. I had no desire to view the floor space. Once they left, Thirteen reentered the room and sat in Eve's spot. I had no plans to start or participate in a conversation, but my host had other plans. She placed her right hand on my left knee. The contact made me uncomfortable and curious as to why she had touched me in this manner. My stomach fluttered. She smiled again. I did not want to offend her, so I let her hand remain. Due in part to my trepidation, I bounced my left foot until her arm shook and she withdrew though she was close enough for me to catch a pleasant smell. Had she sprayed herself with something sweet?

"Nervous?" Thirteen asked me with a devious smile. "Don't be. I won't hurt you."

"This is the end of everything I know," I said.

"Until you fix it."

"That's just it," I sighed. "What if I cannot fix it? What will you do?"

Thirteen chuckled to herself. "Well, for the next two days, I will do whatever I want to do with whomever I want to do it with."

The twinkle in Thirteen's green eyes gave me the impression part of her plans included me, and they should not have. I had never had a romantic or sexual desire for anything or anyone, whether male, female, or non-binary, my entire life. Not that a person should not be attracted to Thirteen. Though they had no physical warmth between them that I'd seen, Thirteen and Nine, I imagined, had done well for themselves, and she would not have expressed interest in me under different circumstances. A part of me was curious, though, what being romantically touched was like. I was appealing to Thirteen, for whatever reason, and the stirring in my belly might be because of her. I had never gotten the opportunity to like or dislike anything—whatever I received was what I must accept.

Thirteen lunged for me and, eyes open, pressed her lips against mine. I froze for a second and did not move. Gradually her lips parted and, in a way, massaged mine. She closed her eyes, but I did not close mine. Her lips were firm and damp with warm moisture. I mimicked what she did with her mouth with a different rhythm. I had done it! I made a choice on my own, and while it was not the most terrible thing I had experienced, I had no feelings from it.

A second later, it was over.

Thirteen wiped her lips with the back of her left hand. "Did you like it?" she asked.

I looked toward my feet and lied so as not to hurt her feelings though my lips tingled. "Yes."

Nine and Eve returned to the room, and I pretended like my first kiss with anyone had not happened.

"We will be comfortable," Eve announced. "His friend will be here soon to review where we are to go and when we are to do it."

Eve sat to my right with Thirteen to my left. Nine would prepare victuals for the five of us. All our meals came from packages, so waiting for any type of sustenance to be prepared was a foreign concept. What did one do in the meantime? There was no work for Eve to busy herself with, and I had no reason to steal. Finally, I broke the silence with a question to Thirteen. "What do you know about the festival?"

"There will be everything," she said. "Music, food, fornication, violent crimes, illegal substances, fornication. No restraint. Whatever feels good to the people, they will do it."

I repeated her statement from earlier. "Whatever they want to do with whomever they want to do it with."

"Or *to*," she added. "The droids are expected to be decommissioned."

Eve said, "I cannot believe the ruling class will lay down and die with the rest of humanity. They must have an escape plan. Another world perhaps?"

Nine shouted from the other chamber. "Another planet? There has not been a comprehensive space program for decades."

Thirteen gave a voice command for their entryway to open. "Greetings, Two."

We turned around to see him. In stepped a bald man with reddish-brown skin and a heavy gray and white beard. Sweat dotted his forehead and ran down his temples. He paused at the sight of us. *"Mongrel women?"* His voice lilted with shock. "You want to sneak mongrel women into the capital library? Are you mad, Thirteen? And Nine, you as well? This will never work."

"It must work, friend," Thirteen said. "This represents our last hope." He huffed. "Last hope? You are supposed to wait until the party to do illegal substances, not leading up to it. This is suicide!"

"We are sober-minded, Two," she retorted. "The map?"

"Right."

Two produced a small, black object between his thumb and forefinger and dropped it in Thirteen's palm. Thirteen, in turn, grabbed my left wrist and placed the object in a port on my smartwatch's bottom that I had never even noticed. With prompting, a hologram of 257's entire layout emerged and projected in front of us. He tapped the inside of the tallest building at the city's center, and it glowed red. "This is the capitol library's entrance," he said. "During the festival, you will be working under the assumption that the main perimeter defenses will be down, and you will be able to enter the main building here. Not many people would want to read anything in the middle of a boisterous party."

Nine brought two platters of food I could not identify. I ate in the manner the others ate. The first object was seasoned and sweet, and the second reminded me of fish but it was round, thick, and flavorful.

"Perimeter defenses will not be a problem," said Nine, still chewing.

Two sucked his teeth. "Right, you can hack those. The main building has droids on the outside of the edifice and human guards on every level's entrance. You need the historical files on the seventh level. Biometric control only. Even should you disarm the series-R droids and the guards, you will have to persuade a soldier to lend you his hand and eyes. Incidentally, what small army are you taking with you to accomplish this?"

I kept quiet.

"The four of you?" he guessed.

"It will work," Eve said. "It must."

"Then, there must be something I am missing, because otherwise, I would say you are signing up for early death. If it's all the same to you, I would prefer to wait."

Nine offered another fish round to his friend, who gladly accepted. "I'd never ask you to take part in anything I did not believe in doing."

"Nor would you have to," Two said with a full mouth. A bit of fish flew from his mouth and landed on the table. "It will be five, now. When do we leave?"

Thirteen suggested a few hours after the festival had begun. Everyone agreed, and Two took his leave. The droid sweeps would begin soon, and as Nine and Thirteen lived on the outer region of the section with the rest of the lower class, their compound would be searched first. The scans were near the same time each day but, according to Thirteen, the buzzing sound signaling its advent came without warning.

Eve and I lined up next to one another with our backs against the hidden wall. I could feel the temperature drop through my suit.

"The compartment will quickly slam closed when I prompt it," Nine said. "The scan will take thirty seconds. Inhale deeply and count backwards from thirty. It will pass quickly." Nine prepared to shut the enclosure.

Soon, we all heard the buzzing in the apartment to the left. True to Nine's word, the scan was over in a flash. Ours would conclude in a similar fashion. We inhaled, Nine placed a palm on the panel to our right, and the door closed.

Thirty.

My mask formed over my head and displayed a blinking reminder about my low oxygen intake level. I disregarded it as I would be breathing soon.

Twenty.

Holding my breath in the dark with a mask on was more difficult than I thought it would be. Was I imagining things, or was Eve's left hand twitching? Stretching out

137

my right pinky, I touched her trembling thumb. What was wrong?

Ten.

Not long now. My chest was burning with the urge to breathe. I counted backward from ten. *Nine, eight, seven, six, five, four, three, two, one!*

Nothing happened. We were still trapped.

I cocked my elbows and pushed my hands forward. The panel would not give. Any excess noise we made would alert authorities to our presence, but if we did not get oxygen soon, it would not matter.

My thoughts overlapped. I clenched my fist and opened a portal in front of us. Eve did not move. I looped my arm around her waist and threw my weight forward. We tumbled into the Narrow Space and fell into the exit portal I had created. When we emerged, she was facedown on the floor, and I lay on top of her back. Nine helped me up, and Thirteen tended to Eve.

"Are you all right, Amirah?" Nine asked.

I gasped for breath. Thirteen pumped her hand on Eve's chest until she jerked forward and coughed. "What...happened?"

"The droids scanned us three times," Nine said. "We thought you were dead." Thirteen's eyes fixed on me. "Why aren't you? What did you do?"

"I brought us here," I told her. Somehow, I thought Nine had told her about us and our abilities while he had us waiting outside. "I can—"

"She knows about your portals. That's not why she's asking you."

"Then, what is it, Nine?"

Thirteen cleared her throat. "The droids left an hour ago."

ELEVEN

T*he future.*

There would be no vaporizing our alternate selves because we had never been here before...here being an hour from when we left.

Nine served us water and encouraged us to sip, but my enthusiasm for water overtook reason, and I swallowed it so fast I choked on it. Thirteen rubbed my back, and while the kneading soothed my muscles, I felt the romantic intent in her strong fingers. Unaware of what else might compel her to stop touching me, I asked to relieve myself. Thirteen volunteered to show me their facilities. I followed her to a small room with a commode, reflective glass, and washing station.

As it turned out, I had to use it. Once I finished, I washed my hands and splashed water on my face. Marveling at free-flowing water, I repeated my actions until wetness dripped from my chin into the metal receptacle. Suddenly, a kind of haze overtook my mind. I took a nootropic from my belt, cupped my hand beneath the water's flow, and brought my hand to my lips. After I swallowed the pill rather than chewing it, the mental fog dissipated, and I reclaimed control of my thoughts.

I had gone to the future. A moment past the one in which I currently lived—I had never ventured to think much ahead of the present. Had we ventured too far forward, we might have ended up floating in Earth's radioactive debris, but I wondered if everything would unfold exactly the way Nine, Thirteen, and Two predicted it.

"Amirah?" Eve, her voice still raspy, called to me from behind the door. "Are you all right?"

"Yes." I left the room. She followed after me and took quite a bit longer.

Nine escorted us to another hidden compartment in the ceiling. Instead of taking us elsewhere to rest, as was the original plan, he insisted we remain close. The utility light in the triangular space's corner cast a small light orb. Eve lay on a cushioned pad closest to it while I lay next to her. Neither of us had space to fully stretch out or sit up straight without encountering a barrier. We crimped our bodies inside as best we could. "Do not come down until one of us beckons you," he said, the creases in his face stretched thin. "Even if your bowels constrict."

They had not moved today, and now I was concerned.

"Good night," Nine said.

Eve and I had never wished one another anything prior to retiring for any evening. On the cusp of the world ending, however, with my world near its end, I wished her a good night. She returned my sentiment. My body sank into the cushion's plush fibers. Even with my eyes closed, I could not clear my thoughts long enough to sleep although this might be my last chance to do so before the end. I whispered, "Almunashiy" until Eve stirred and mumbled, "What is it?"

"Should I succeed tomorrow, what will become of you? Will I never see you again?"

The pitch-black space prevented us from seeing one another, but I imagined her bottom lip folded inward the way it did before she delivered hard truths.

Her considerable pause was more than I could bear. Tears welled in my eyes and dropped past my temples wetting my ears. My breaths hitched, and burning ebbed in my chest. Of course. Before the world became *this,* it was intact; the planet had a thriving population and would have no need for cloning. Outside of my lifetime, I would

THE DOOMSDAY CLOCK

be surrounded by more people than I had ever known and completely alone.

"Will you go with me?" I asked her.

More lip-folded silence. No doubt her reasons had to do with preserving timeline integrity and creating more branched realities that I cared nothing about. I *needed* Almunashiy, the person who created me, raised me, and gave me knowledge, not Eve. "There will be no need for me any longer," she said.

"No."

"Beyond both our lifetimes. Your success...everything we have known. Everyone we have ever met, including one another...we will cease to exist to you." After a considerable pause, she said, "I don't remember much about my childhood home. My first memory is the scent of synthetic milk rationed to us after the 2035 incident. I *envy* you for that, One."

"Why?"

"You can record my appearance, my voice. I will always be with you."

I blinked away tears. Unbeknownst to her, I had been doing just that since we left Vagrant City. *But did she love me?* I finally asked her the question. "Do you love me?"

Following another protracted silence, Eve admitted, "I don't know how. No one has ever loved me."

"That's not true, Almunashiy," I mumbled past the free-flowing streams from my eyes. "That's not true."

"Then you have surpassed my understanding, and I have failed you in this."

A lifetime of pressing emotions below the surface had taken its toll on me. I cried without conscience, fear of judgment, or consequence. My guardian did not scold or comfort me. My sobbing became sniffing and mild convulsions. Any more noise than this would reveal our location.

We did not speak for a while.

"There was once this organization that invented the Doomsday Clock," Eve whispered. "It believed that the human race would become the author of its future cataclysmic destruction. What time is it on your Doomsday Clock now?"

Her tone was neither sarcastic nor bitter. I had long joked about it, and now that I knew the truth, I failed to see the humor in it as well. "An hour until midnight."

She did not say anything more. I knew the answers. Even with the nootropic, my memories of the previous time I had gone backward and forward in time existed like vague dreams in my consciousness. Pressing myself to

144

remember specifics, I could conjure up the emotional importance of what I had seen and done but no details. The first instance had to do with Eight. Something terrible had happened to Eight in the other reality. Today, I had gone forward in time changing nothing. Those remembrances were fresher in my recollection. I still recalled the coldness inside the secret chamber.

From the day I would exit in the past, gradually, they would all skirt the fringes of my enhanced memory until all the people I had ever grown to care about would disappear. In 215, loss was a constant certainty. The first thing about a deceased person to fade from my memory was their voice. Next, everything else would go away until all that remained were whispers of past interactions and the emotions related to them.

I could not wander this path alone. I would not.

I conjured a portal to my left and rolled my body into it so quickly Eve did not have an opportunity to stop me. I needed some time to think. The Omnikhron's exit point was the entrance of our old compound. I found myself swallowed by a sandstorm. The ramp lowered, and I ran inside, securing it behind me. Another government lie. It had not been razed as previously advertised. On the cusp of being extinct, who could bother with a handful of people destined to die anyway?

Shaking the dust from my body, I panted. Our quarters smelled terrible, like decaying flesh and a cesspool of excrement. Breathing through my mouth extended the disgust to my tongue. It was all I could do not to retch and vomit over the grated floor. And, it could have been my imagination, but was there movement in Almunashiy's quarters? Had it been a droid, I would have been long dead.

"Who's there?" Her ragged voice was familiar.

"Eight."

She maneuvered to a sitting position on my mentor's mattress. She was now a skeleton with sagging, sore-pocked red skin covering her bones.

"One," she groaned. "You have hair now. And a *hand*?"

I dared not approach closer due to the nauseating stench. "It is a long story. What happened to you? What are you doing here?"

"My shelter, the Hub, Twenty-Three's compound—all gone. Yours I had access to." She waved her bony hand. "No food or water. Too drained to leave. And if I could, where would I go? Here is as good a place as any."

To die, she meant. She came back to 215 to die.

"Where have you come from? And what have you brought me?"

The story about how I came to be here—Vagrant City, its destruction, my name and body changes, meeting

Nine, entering 454, and fleeing—was long and winding. I gave facts, and when her jaundiced eyes flitted, I assumed she had questions, so I added details.

With a hacking cough and her limbs violently shaking, Eight pointed a finger at me. She tried speaking although I could not understand the words through the wet rattle in her throat. Had the information upset her? She had left my company long ago, not the other way around, and in doing so, she condemned herself to this current state.

Did she think it was my fault?

Perhaps it was. I could have forced her hand. Not like she could have run or hidden from me. I could have checked on her in the present without disrupting the time flow or meeting a copy of myself. Between fleeing my hometown and changing my identity, I had not considered it.

An Omnikhron appeared between me and Eight. Had I unconsciously done that? I clenched my fist to close it with no success. Again, I clenched my fist, squeezing my fingers to the stinging point. Nothing. I had not noticed before, but the portal rotated to my right—opposite the direction of mine. My heart skipped a beat.

The assassin had come for me.

Spreading my fingers wide, I opened my own portal behind me. A hand reached through and yanked me forward off balance into the Narrow Space. The building pressure in my skull was too much to bear. I collapsed to my knees and coughed into nothingness. My tongue and eyes sizzled. Thankfully, my bodysuit formed around my body to protect me from asphyxiation.

Finally. I found myself at the feet of someone. No sense in fleeing since they knew enough to find me in the first place and had powers similar to or more powerful than my own. They kicked at my hands. Until the burning in my body subsided, I had trouble trying to stand. I made it to one knee then gradually straightened my back.

Our suits glowed the same iridescent purple. We were similar, if not exactly the same, in height and build. The only difference was their right wrist ended in a rounded stub like my left had formerly done. Realization weighed my heart and, as if they knew what I thought, they nodded.

Something had gone terribly wrong for this to happen.

This, Almunashiy warned me, must *never* happen.

I could not come into direct contact with a living version of myself.

One thing that made sense was she dragged me here into the Narrow Space. Maybe the rules did not apply here? She tapped her left ear with her index finger. Of course. I mimicked the motion until the comms switched to a channel where I heard mumbling in my own voice that was not from me.

Coming face-to-face with myself overwhelmed me. I gasped. It *was* true. Here, apparently, quantum physics did not apply—at least not with immediate consequences. "H-how?"

Her voice sparked with interest as if I should have remembered something so impactful yet did not. "I knew, in time, you would return to 215. I recalled the date, not the time. Thank you for not making me wait forever. Nice hand, by the way."

"You chose not to replace..."

"Not my style."

"How then did you lose–"

"—loneliness on both our parts."

"Stop completing my sentences. How–"

"We don't have–"

"Interrupting me! Stop interrupting me!"

"I know what you are going to say, and it is difficult to wait with so little time–"

"How did you lose your hand?"

"How did *we* lose our hands? You were three years old. You cast a portal to a future time, *my time*, by mistake. I held your hand. When Almunashiy returned, and you escaped, I did not let go."

She raised her right wrist's stump. She had not let go of me, and my closing Omnikhron had severed our hands. I shuddered at the idea of me, as a child, severing my hand in this manner. Examining my own wrist, I saw the line where the fusion had occurred, but the skin texture on the new growth felt artificial. I suppose she did not mean to sound as psychotic as she did.

My heads-up display flashed a warning about my 120-beat-per-minute heart rate. "You did not stay."

She shook her head. "And I cannot now. The event horizon's particles are unstable. You feel it, too. Unsteadiness is growing in your mind, peeling back the layers of your sanity, what you understand, and what you thought you knew. Your limbs, like mine, are hurting from the strain. Again, we don't have much time here."

Indeed. I crossed my arms to steady my hands. Bones were inflexible, yet the sensations I experienced were that they stretched and bent. My doppelgänger balled her fists. From the looks of it, we were suffering the same fate. "Tomorrow, you will fail."

"I must try."

Her tone dripped condescension. "Of course. *Try*. I am proof of your future failure. But go ahead. The effort alone may kill you. Attempt what I could not do six times. Succeed where I failed. Stop the nuclear winter."

My stomach clenched. Six times? She had created six alternate timelines? "Surely, I can change the future if I know about it in advance. What must I do?"

"Kill the girl on December 4, 2029."

What? "Kill who? What girl? And why—"

"Apparently, we can kill a copy of ourselves with little hesitation. Another person is a different story..."

She had murdered five times to eliminate the paradox.

"Overcome the universal self-correction, eliminate one life over *billions*—"

Her speech hitched, I guessed, from the agony of maintaining the wormhole. My own breaths were difficult to catch. What I heard was disconnected nonsense. If the stress from time leaping almost sixty years into the past might kill me, what more had it done to her after so many attempts? Nerves in the middle of my back cinched, and I hunched over. My suit's oxygen supply lowered to ten percent, sending a warning to my display. In sixty seconds, I would run out of purified air.

Still, in the midst of dizziness, I managed to utter, "Whose life?" As in, if I made it to the destination, what was the identity of the person whose life I must take?

She fell to one knee, her suit's lighting sputtering. The date and location flashed in my suit's heads-up display— about sixty years ago. I recognized the name of the location from the little historical studying I'd done on classified government documents. The GPS coordinates pointed to what looked like a military installation. My doppelgänger said this was my last chance to intervene without causing more damage with another branched timeline.

I cast open a gateway and waved goodbye to her. She collapsed in a ball, and without her efforts, too, I could no longer remain in the Narrow Space.

I escaped, not to my home, but back in the crawlspace with Eve. My mask retracted into the suit, and by the time I came back to myself, I felt wetness below my nose and on the sides of my neck. Blood. I coughed, and more spurted from my mouth and splashed back onto my face.

Thankfully, Nine opened the compartment, cursed upon viewing my current state, and helped me down.

"She's hemorrhaging," Eve said as I gagged. "Help her!"

Thirteen appeared with wet towels and cleaned me. Still groggy from my experience, I knew from the lilt in their voices, though I could not make out their words, that our benefactors wanted to know what had happened to me. My words came out in incomprehensible mumbles, but Eve told them I had disappeared for most of the night and reappeared in the morning. She correctly theorized that, though she had barely slept, nighttime had passed normally for the three of them. Meanwhile, I had skipped over that period and returned in what amounted to a few moments to me.

After an intravenous disc of nutrients and fluids, a chance to wash, and a change of clothing, I felt something close to normal. The pounding headache had waned to a mild throb, and my limbs had steadied. Watching myself in the looking glass, I mouthed random words. My speech and voice had returned, but the gaps in my memory reminded me to take a nootropic.

Suddenly, my mind reached equilibrium and clarity. I remembered the date my older version had given me.

December 4, 2029.

With no specific time, I postulated midnight might well be my best chance not to miss anything. However, I would need time to recover from the journey, and without anyone to help me, I would have to figure this out alone.

As existential as it sounded, I wondered whether or not I could trust *myself*. Granted, a different version of me, but me. What reason could I have to lie, to send myself toward an unknown type of destruction?

Nine and Thirteen offered us breakfast. There were mostly foods I did not recognize, but still, I devoured everything served to me, strange colors, textures, and tastes notwithstanding. While we ate, measured explosions popped in the distance.

"Ah!" Nine raised his glass in a salute. "The celebration festival has begun! Perhaps some of the choice opiates and intoxicants will still be available by the time we arrive."

At the meal's conclusion, I sensed our discussion should pivot to an explanation regarding what had happened to me last night. The thing was, even with a clear mind, I barely understood them myself. I gave it my best.

Thirteen clasped her fingers together and shook them. "So, this *other version* of you–"

"Temporal paradox."

"All right, Eve. This temporal paradox gave you a date by which to kill a girl? And that murder will prevent this hellscape from occurring in the first place?"

Eve violently shook her head. "To her, not to us. That is not how time travel works. This reality remains for us."

Nine and Thirteen laughed, presumably at us. "Our mistake," said Thirteen, a smile lingering on her lips. "He and I were under the impression that traveling through time was an unbelievable collection of impossible, untested theories. Until last night, that is."

"When Amirah goes back to that event, any future she realizes from that critical point in time until the day she dies is *her* reality. Here, our reality without her will end as it is supposed to."

Nine tapped his finger against his temple. "But does it have to?"

I was confused.

"If she returns to this time in this reality...nothing will have changed for us? All of us still perish?"

"Yes." Eve said.

"And she," Thirteen said, pointing at me, "will not return to our reality?"

There was no hiding the gravity and grief in my voice. "No."

Nine clapped his hands together. "Then, we will go with you to the past!"

TWELVE

"We will not!" Eve's voice thundered throughout the room. "Did you forget about her hemorrhage from this morning?"

Her words sapped the breath from my lungs and stabbed in my chest. *Hemorrhage?* That explained the metallic taste lingering in my mouth and the sensation of a clot stuck in the back of my throat no matter how much I drank.

The nootropics Seraphina had supplied us with were a day away from expiring. Soon, I would forget all that I had learned. But I knew what had to be done. Almunashiy, or Eve, must accompany me. I needed her indomitable strength. Nine and Thirteen had been hospitable, welcomed us into their home, and hidden us from droids.

I did not know that meant I should add odds to further risk my life and bring them into the past, did it?

"She makes a salient point, my love." Thirteen sounded compassionate even if she was not. "We will live our last moments in debauchery and hedonism, and perhaps, when our souls depart for the universal unknown, we will live again."

Nine sighed and nodded resignation. "Rest," he commanded me. "Recuperate. Have run of our home. We will return to see you off, Amirah."

Eve rose and helped me stretch my frame out on the furniture while Nine and Thirteen retreated to another room. I dozed off and awoke to the couple leaving the home. Thirteen was barely dressed—the tops of her breasts and her smooth alabaster legs and back were visible. I doubted she wore undergarments. Similarly, Nine was bare chested, smothered in red, blue, and purple paint, and covered at the crotch. The festival had to have some type of temperature- and weather-control mechanism for him to be dressed this way.

My eyes were barely cracked open, and I hoped they would assume I was asleep and leave. Not long afterward, I drifted off for real. My dreams were loud, vivid, and bright—a blend of what I had seen before and what I feared most—broken skeletons, purple ash, violent, belching black skies, and pooling blood.

Eve awoke me, her hands forcefully clamped down over my biceps. "You must go alone. Do not return to this time."

I blinked hard and mumbled. "What?"

She deadlifted me from the furniture and placed me onto my feet. A tugging at my midsection alerted me that she was jamming her nootropics into my belt.

I had thought my imagination had taken over, and my dream had had its own nightmare, but no, *the earth was shaking on its own*. Like when the droids attacked Vagrant City, but we were above ground this time. These tremors were less rhythmic and far more violent.

The final destruction had begun. Thirteen and Nine's apartment had begun tearing itself apart. The wooden and glass housewares hung on the wall fell and shattered. Their holographic screens followed suit. My heart raced and pounded.

More time. I needed more time. With her. With *this*. I could go back into the past forever and not have enough.

I took hold of her hands. "Come with me," I pleaded.

To my surprise, she squeezed my fingers. "It is not my place. You will go alone."

I yelled her name and cursed. I had never cursed at her face. "Please?"

"No, and do not come back."

Tears dropped from my eyes. "You do not understand. Without you, I do not have the strength—"

"Amirah—"

"I can't go without *you*. I love you."

"One—"

"We will go with you," Nine said.

Neither of us had noticed Thirteen and Nine had returned. Thirteen held Ordnance trained at Eve's back. The bright makeup on her face had been smeared, and both of them brought a pungent scent back with them. The little clothing Nine wore was stained. "The more we thought about it, we decided to live another day. You will assist us in this."

"No. You said…"

She unloaded an Ordnance shot into Eve's back. Eve dropped to her knees and fell facedown onto the floor. Without hesitation, she sent a kill shot through Nine's temple. He, too, slumped to the ground. A sudden coldness hit at my core. I should have trusted my senses about Nine and Thirteen and their intentions once they found out what I could do.

My heart dropped. They were One World. They had to be.

Eve was dead, a small, smoking hole burrowed into her lower back. From this point forward, I would trust no one.

"Like I told you, whatever I want to do with whomever I want to do it with." Despite my protests, she forcefully kissed me and rubbed the still-hot Ordnance barrel against my scalp. "You should consider doing the same. Now, let's not make more of a mess of things, hmm? We will do beautiful things together. Open the gateway."

Still facing one another, I stared wordlessly at Eve's unmoving body. For me, the earthquake, the ongoing solar flares, the yawning metal, and the cracking wood all vanished. Although she denied knowing how to do so, she did love me in her own way.

"Umiy" I muttered to her in Arabic. *Mother. The only one I would know.*

I would die here and now if it meant we would simultaneously go into the afterlife, but knowing Thirteen, she would spare me out of spite for disobeying her. When the next tremor hit and lasted long enough to distract Thirteen, I focused on the date I needed to go to, December 4, 2029, and commanded a portal to open.

Immediately, all the pain from last night returned. Blood streamed from my nose, and fiery agony ripped through both sides of my brain. I screamed from the back of my throat. The wormhole's structure squeezed and expanded. Its instability seemed to originate with the pain, and once it eased, the doorway widened.

I could feel Thirteen's eyes behind me. She was coming.

Before Thirteen could circle me and enter the Omnikhron, Eve sprung to her feet, and, in one motion, pushed me through the portal and threw Thirteen backward. She shielded me from the rapid Ordnance fire bursts. Thirteen would die there, but so would Eve.

The last memory I would have of my mother figure was of her falling facedown to her death, her back smoking from laser fire and succumbing to her injuries.

I did not remember opening the second portal to exit.

Was I dead?

If nerve endings had voices, mine would be shouting, "Die, and get it over with." Everything was agony, especially my head. I was lying flat on my back, arms by my sides, feet upright. Cocking my head forward to get a view of the rest of me was not possible. To my sides was whiteness—no apertures—a sealed container of a place. What I could feel surrounding my skin resembled my bodysuit.

My destination in the past was a military installation. and were this truly the first quarter of the twenty-first century, whoever discovered me might want to dissect the mongrel girl who just fell out of a glowing blue interdimensional portal.

My chest burned with my last memory before coming here. Eve, Almunashiy, the one I called Mama before her death had called me *bint* or daughter. I had called her *umiy* or *mother*. She had sacrificed her life to save mine.

And then, she died.

Giving in to thirst, despair, and fatigue, I fell asleep wishing never to wake up.

My cheeks stung with needles as if they had been slapped. "Who are you?" someone with a gruff, male voice asked. The source was outside of my peripheral vision and beyond my perspective.

"One!" I shouted to stop the hurting.

"Who are you?"

I repeated the same thing until I realized he was not a series-R droid, and this was not 2084. "Amirah," I mumbled. The speed at which I moved my lips did not match that of what I said in my brain. "Amirah Mostafa."

Despite my confusion, I was completely calm with a steady heart rate and pulse. For good or bad reasons, I concluded I was being drugged.

I was not completely naked, but my suit was gone, replaced by something thin, soft, and loose fitting. Mobility had returned to my neck muscles, but a thick bind below my chin immobilized my head save for a few degrees of mobility. The bind chafed my skin as I struggled to move. To my left was a machine of some sort, less sophisticated than I had ever seen but similar in that it measured vital signs. The one with the ancient symbol for heart could be my heart rate—if so, seventy-six was not terrible. The fraction, blood pressure, one hundred twenty over eighty.

Everything was normal.

A tube rested between my thighs. They had catheterized me. Meaning I had been unconscious long enough not to have controlled my bladder.

Immediately, my pulse spiked. The machine's beeping corresponded with my rising anxiety.

Had I been operated on? What had they done?

"Easy."

This time the voice was softer, calmer. I assumed it belonged to a female. "How...long?" I managed to croak.

"How long have you been unconscious? You've been in and out for three days. We found you on the front steps."

No. Almunashiy had died in vain. I had gone to the past and, because of my weakness, passed out and missed my window. My chin stung above the bind as I tearfully turned my head in disbelief. I felt a prick in the bend of my left arm and then a cool sensation ebbed from the spot. The beeping slowed, and the ceiling whiteness became fuzzy. I saw a pale-white blurry face with red or orange hair I could not tell for sure—and the person shined a bright light into my eyes one at a time.

"I think I gave her too much," she said.

The person with the deeper voice from before said, "Ask her."

At this point, I would answer anything. My hope was gone.

"Amirah Mostafa's name and fingerprints do not register on any known database on the planet. Who are you *really?*"

I responded with the only other option. "1-13-9-18-1-8."

She sighed and leaned to where I could have clearly seen her facial features had I not been dosed with a drug. "If that's supposed to be your social security number, 113-91-818…you're missing a number. Run all permutations of

164

that number," she said to someone I could not see. "Where are you from? Your accent is not showing regional dialectal markings our language program can detect."

It was getting harder to talk intelligibly with whatever drug relaxing my muscles including my tongue. "S-sector 215," I slurred.

"Pennsylvania? That area code is for Pennsylvania. You are from Pennsylvania?"

What is a Pennsylvania? "No. I do not know."

"We are getting nowhere," she said to the man I could not see. "She's fading. I gave her too much."

"Try," he insisted. "Ask her before she passes out."

"A couple of days ago, someone who looks exactly like you with a missing right hand and a buzzed haircut stepped through a blue circle with readings akin to a black hole and nearly killed a young girl on the East Coast." My doppelgänger. One of the times she had failed in her mission. "Girl."

"How did you do it?"

I barely understood how temporal paradoxes worked, I was under the influence of some kind of narcotic that made me incredibly fatigued, and she expected me to explain it? "Not me...really."

Even in doing so, my mission would not have changed. I would have to succeed where my temporal paradox had failed and murder the girl she talked about, perhaps her and the man, too, if they got in my way, to save the planet.

Oh, how I wished Almunashiy were here to advise me! She might not even have had an answer for my dilemma, but her presence in the face of uncertainty had always soothed me.

Without a nootropic in my system, straight line thinking and reasoning were a longer process. Perhaps, if I told her it *was* me, they would relieve me of the responsibility of doing this. Who knew anymore? What did I have left to lose? "Not...me...identi...fication number...1-13-9-18-1-8..."

She incorrectly repeated my number again. "You're missing a number, and every combination brings up someone who's not you."

"And I was cloned...in the year 2066."

She paused. I was not sure if it was because I said cloned, 2066, or both.

"You're..."

I nodded the best I could. From the future.

PART TWO

THIRTEEN

Once the medicine took full effect and lured me unconscious, I slumbered again for who knew how long. Without my smartwatch—useless without calibration to their equivalent of the world's clock—or the heads-up display in my bodysuit mask, I had no concept of time or the Doomsday Clock, as it were. In my former life, that would not have bothered me. But, here and now, it meant *everything*. Instead of preventing the future I had come from, now, I might be doomed to watch it manifest.

When I blinked awake this time, a Black woman had replaced the reddish-orange-haired woman who had been tending to me. "Good morning," she said. Her pleasant voice rang with warmth.

I licked my cracking lips and looked around. The rectangular room was almost all white, save for silver instruments I did not recognize. "Is it morning?" I asked.

"Indeed."

Rarely had I considered another human being beautiful. But *she*...her skin was several shades darker than mine and smoother without the gray sores and pocks customary on 215 residents. I had also never seen straight hair on a person her color before. Fine, dark brown, and with an unmistakable sheen, it had been combed and rolled into a ball at the back of her head. Her brown eyes and facial expressions spoke of an inner sadness. I wondered what the source of it might be.

She added a bag of clear liquid to a pole beside the bed and connected it to the tube in my arm. "Time for breakfast." She flicked the bottom with her finger, I presumed, to move the flow along. "It's not bacon and eggs, but it'll do."

Bacon? Eggs? "What happened to...?"

"While you were out, you kept mumbling in Arabic the words for creator and mother. It was thought that I may be a better fit to attend to you since I understood the language. I studied it for a few years."

Almunashiy had *died* for me. I felt a burning prick in my heart. Her death could not be in vain. "Where am I? What year is this really?"

The woman crossed her arms at the wrists. "You understand why I won't tell you, right? Giving a time traveler information like that would be extremely dangerous."

My eyes bulged. "You *believe* me?"

"We interfaced with your nanotech bodysuit, and small rudiments of its design are rooted in our models. The data stored also backs up your story. So, yes, I believe you are from the future, Amirah—more than your word, the science supports it."

Relief washed over my limbs, and my muscles relaxed. It was not everything, but perhaps, a small step toward me accomplishing what I came here to do was securing the faith of another. "How long will I be confined in this place?"

"You are severely dehydrated. You have jaundice, vitamin deficiencies across the board, and you're borderline anemic. If I unplugged your intravenous feed and freed you this second, you would not make it to the hallway."

In 215, none of those maladies were out of the ordinary. "That is not all," I surmised.

"Now that we know who you are, *why* are you here?"

170

"Where and when is *here?*" I shot back. "I am not sure I am even in the right year, or month, or day for it to be relevant."

My caretaker repositioned her body at a strange angle above mine and silently mouthed, "What year?"

"Twenty twenty-nine," I mouthed back.

"That's not information that I can give you," she announced. From the slight smirk across her lips and the way her cheekbones rose, I surmised I was in the correct year.

I had made it.

◼•●●●•◼

Their treatments strengthened me in ways I could never have imagined. The constant cramping and hunger pains in my stomach subsided. Then, they weaned me from the clear intravenous cocktail and served me actual food, which was delicious. I found myself to have a natural affinity for fowl, vegetables, and red-skinned fruits. The muscle fiber's strings caught in my teeth, which I had been taught to eliminate through flossing, and the fruits alternated between sweet and tart flavors. Also, they did some drilling in my mouth that cured the pain but left my teeth extra sensitive to hot and cold.

Meanwhile, my caretaker, who still had not revealed her name nor anything I could call her, bathed me each day with a soft, holey surface called a sponge until I could do so on my own. I settled on calling her Miss, considering you was impolite. When I became independent, after blindfolding and deafening me first, Miss took me to a facility to cleanse myself. She made it a point to suppress my abilities, how, I was not sure. Not that I tried to escape. But the vitality that invigorated my blood was gone. Where would I even go? I did not know where or when I was, and the trip here had nearly killed me.

The clothes I now wore were gray and soft but stiff against my skin, which needed constant lubrication to keep from bleeding. The thick substance they used smelled pleasant and gave my body a high shine. My shoes were the same color cloth with a rigid, white, flexible material for the sole. Ushered from place to place, I could not see nor hear, and with my hands bound, I could not remedy either. For now, my mission to prevent the world's destruction was behind me and unattainable. I had to become content with safety from imminent death, consistent cleanliness, and not active starvation.

To avoid becoming indolent, I asked for the opportunity to exercise and received permission and private access to a weight room containing metal machines providing resistance to my movements. Still, I had not encountered another human besides my caretaker. Miss instructed me on which muscle groups to focus on in order to build endurance, which I had in limited supply. Afterward, my sore muscles screamed for relief and my lungs burned. Apparently, this was normal.

Back in my room, for I had been in it long enough to claim partial ownership of it, I lay on my bed and started thinking about my purpose—not why I came here in the first place, but why were they keeping me alive? For what reason did they need me alive and healthy? I kept coming back to one thing. Because I had appeared in the past, they knew the nature of my abilities. So, it made sense they might want me for the same reason Nine and Thirteen did—as a weapon to point at a target.

"What do I call you?" I said to Miss as she checked my vital signs.

She paused and then said, "Miss, what you've been calling me, is fine."

"Why are you keeping me alive, Miss?"

No answer.

The machine monitoring my pulse accelerated. "What is the exact date, Miss?" I demanded. "Why am I here? *Why am I here?*"

Miss attempted to restrain me by herself and could not. Although she threw her weight against my wrists, I kicked free with abandon and thrashed enough to free myself from her grasp. That was when I saw the impossible. Now, not one Miss held me down, but four of them did. She was a quadruplet? How did I miss their entrance? I stood no chance against them all, and while three of them restrained my body, the fourth sedated me. My vision blurred, and I fell unconscious.

When I awoke, I was restrained again at the wrists and ankles. They had also dressed my hands in rigid gloves to prevent me from making a fist. Though my physical condition was the best it ever had been and my constant headaches had subsided, I feared my blood vessels would explode. Did she know this? I could not let on. I had grown too familiar with Miss; after all, she was my captor, nothing more.

I had lost more time, how much, I could not be sure. My captors were diligent about bathing and shaving me, so I could not tell by the itchiness in my armpits or lack thereof. Losing the concept of time had gradually untied my grip on reality, which was tenuous to begin with. Without regular doses of the nootropic, I had forgotten so much of what I had learned in...Vagrant City. Glowing water and screaming, oh, the hoarse, awful, terrible screaming. I would never forget it. Bits of information like that floated beyond my mental grasp, and it was a struggle to catch them.

Miss patted me on the shoulder. "How are you feeling—a little drowsy? We tapered off the sedative quite a while ago. I'm not sure why it affected you this way."

The pleasant platitudes did nothing to soften my resolve. She reached for my restraints, I assumed, to tighten them. Instead, to my surprise, she unlocked them and removed the rigid gloves. My skin had red imprints and chafing from the binds. With my knuckles cracking, I rubbed the circulation back into my wrists, and I immediately thought of escaping to reunite with Almunashiy in the doomed future.

She clicked her teeth and pointed to my already clenched fist. "Before you do that, there is some information you should have. Those headaches you have been having are small brain bleeds, but the last one you suffered was significant, and you nearly died.

"The increasing strain of your abilities is what causes the hemorrhaging." She stopped talking to clear her throat. "Fifty-five years in the past is a long way. Stick to shorter trips, or the next time you use them in a major way may be the last."

A part of me was relieved the burden of saving the planet might no longer on my shoulders, but then, I would be in indefinite limbo with no purpose. Here, in this world, I did not exist yet, and there was no Almunashiy, no Eight, no Twenty-Three, not even Nine and Thirteen. To these people, Miss especially, I was a lab experiment to deconstruct.

"Am I free to go?" I asked her. "Or, will you and your sisters stop me?"

"Where would you go?"

Back to anything I knew might certainly result in my demise, and although there was presently no larger purpose or direction to my life in this world I did not know, I did not want to toss my life away. "I am of no threat to you or anyone," I said barely above a whisper. "If I go home, I will die in transit or when I arrive. I have nothing."

My doppelgänger was right.

I had failed indeed.

"Even with your abilities, your brain is still healing," said Miss. "Give it some time. You still have that. Which reminds me…" She pulled my smartwatch from her pants pocket. "The advanced tech made this a process to recalibrate, but it's accurate according to Coordinated Universal Time—which is what I believe you were operating on where you are from. We left it that way to make it more comfortable for you. Subtract eight hours, and that is the time here. Change it when you want or don't. As long as there's an internet signal where you are, it'll automatically update."

What's an internet? I clasped the device to my wrist and looked at it.

The display sucked the breath from my lungs. "How long have I been here?" I managed to ask.

"A month."

According to my smartwatch's readings, the date was
January 4, 2030.

FOURTEEN

A *month?*

What became immediately clear was that the irreversible damage to the planet had already started. Without access to my abilities, I was quite harmless. Like Thirteen, Nazirah, and One World before them, they wanted something from me. Between my multiple bouts of unconsciousness, they could have experimented on me or harvested my DNA. The open sores on my body left them plenty of access points, and I would hardly know the difference.

Until I healed enough to be somewhere else, I was trapped. All things considered, my situation, aside from the constant, yawning emptiness in my heart, was not that bad. Like in Vagrant City, I ate on a regular basis and bathed so often my skin ached. What was clear was that I was being used. For what purpose, exactly, was unclear.

When I found out why was being nursed to perfect health, I'd fight for all it was worth. One day, I asked to see the skies, and for the first time, Miss obliged me by taking me someplace without a blindfold. No one else was present, and as I followed her, I had the impulse to run but did not. Someone else here might not recognize me as a patient or gentle prisoner and treat me as kindly.

We stopped in front of a massive rectangular-paned window and watched as radioactive flakes fell. While used to them, I had never seen precipitation this shade of gray before. Also, the clouds above were thin and wispy white, not as thick, dark, and angry as ours.

"This is a season we call winter," she said while pointing at the sky. "But that, that is not snow."

I had failed.

Perhaps, if I recuperated enough, I could jump back a month or so and prevent this from happening again without causing myself further brain damage? I might fail at that, too. And *die*. Why even attempt?

"From what I remember of the historical records, this is how everything began," I said. "What terrible being caused this? It was a person, was it not?"

I watched as Miss's face fell. "Someone like you— someone like you with abilities lost control of them."

"A girl?" *The* girl.

Her pause was all the answer I needed, but she answered anyway. "Yes."

My stomach clenched. This world-destroying person lived, which meant I might be able to stop her from decimating the planet for good. Miss's halting tone indicated she knew much more than she was telling me.

"You feel *sympathy* toward this person? Why?"

"Knowing what we know now from you—"

"A mass murderer who committed genocide on my world."

"—we can prevent that outcome *without killing her.*"

I shook my head. Every muscle in my body tensed. I had felt this way many times before, and Almunashiy warned me to watch my tone and to tamp down my anger. Instead, this time, I allowed the fire within me to swell and rage uncontrolled. "Her death is a definite solution."

"Not necessarily. Not if she cannot die."

I gritted my teeth. *"Everything* can die."

"There's a better way, Amirah."

"And you expect me to join you in this pacifist mission?" I yelled in her face. "You assume too much! Only my home remained, and I left just before she blew that up, too."

"You don't understand, she's—"

180

I pointed to the cloudy sky. "This will happen again and again and again until your land is incinerated, the livestock perishes, crops fail to produce, and the water is poison to drink. You have *no idea* what it is like. You treat water here as if it is worthless! We cherish every drop because we must! Imagine having the choice of bathing, washing clothes, ridding your home of waste, or drinking to survive every day without fail."

Apocalyptic prophecy did nothing to change her mind. The horrors were far too abstract to comprehend. "There must be a better way," she said. "You're right. I did assume. I am asking you...this less murderous version of you...will you help me find it?"

Finally, the reason *why* she nursed me back to health. My visits, past and present, had informed her and her comrades of everything they needed to know about me—my name, background, history, the intricacies of my biology, the tech in my bodysuit and smartwatch—*everything*. Her science had sussed out more about me than anyone alive knew.

I had little left to lose except time, which I now had in abundance. The next devastating nuclear attack would not be for years, and, once I healed, I could change my mind, return earlier, and destroy this person responsible for the nuclear winter.

"Yes. But I need something in return."

A description came to mind of a scene in an old holovision film I had once viewed and secretly envied. A man, woman, and their children sat in chairs stationed around a table. They participated in conversation while sharing a meal consisting of dishes I had never seen before. I imagined the white smoke wafting from the containers smelled pleasant. The best scent I had ever experienced was our protein packets, which had a slight but sharp, seasoned aroma to them.

After hearing my request, she said a quick and decisive "No."

"You can dampen my powers. I will be of no threat."

I could tell her negative resolve was waning by the twisting of her mouth. "No."

"Plus, you have my word."

For all that a promise from a stranger was worth, I expected her to continue denying me. I had asked for a meal at her home. *Home*. She protected the concept of her place of dwelling in a way I never would. What was there to defend—a drained water reservoir, a shabby, four-compartment compound, and the Hub? It was not a lot, but I shared my experiences with her as much as one could about a place they would never see. And honestly, if I happened to meet a girl who could destroy planets, what could I do to her?

Miss returned me to my room where I stayed until the midday meal. Alone, I listlessly dawdled over my food and ate little. Interaction with someone, *anyone*, would have been welcomed. Miss was nowhere to be seen. In the room, I lay back on the bed and made a fist. A small Omnikhron appeared above my hand, and a small dribble of crimson liquid dripped from my nose onto my upper lip. I wiped it off with the back of my left hand, and the red streak startled me enough to close the tiny portal. I could not have fit anything in it larger than my arm. If I was going to do anything to prevent the future or see Almunashiy again, I would need help.

A soft weight landed on my stomach and awoke me. I blinked and saw Miss standing at the foot of the bed. "Let's get you dressed."

I sat up. "For what reason?"

"I changed my mind. We're leaving. You should look a little different if you are coming to my home."

Taking the clothes in my hand, I smiled and quickly undressed. Miss left the room to give me privacy. The pants were soft, black, and clung to my legs. The shirt was thick, warm, and a shade of blue I had never seen before. The black and gray shoes were more rigid than my usual pair and fit tight around my foot coverings called socks, I think. She returned once I was fully dressed. "Ready?" she asked me.

"Yes." My eyes drifted to a metal cuff the width of my finger in her hand.

"Give me your arm," she commanded. "Your word is unfortunately not good enough."

"What is this?" I asked her.

"An insurance policy. It will dampen your abilities and tether you to this reality but not leave you defenseless." She pulled the left sleeve of her white coat back to reveal a bracelet identical to the one she currently locked on my right wrist just above my scar. "Any dramatic spikes in radioactivity would give the government an excuse to kick our doors down."When she snapped the metal around my right wrist, I immediately felt the difference in my body. My energy level lowered, and fatigue overcame me.

We walked side by side down multiple corridors until we approached a portion of the building with yellow and black symbols. I recognized them. Radiation. The click of her shoes against the floor quickened, and I matched her walking pace. Assuming the girl she insisted protecting caused this, she understood, on a small level, what I came from. Most parts of my world's remaining sectors were hospitable except the outer boundaries, which no one bothered approaching.

"Why would the government 'kick down your doors'?"

"Control. A stealth but mobile thinking weapon would be invaluable in a lot of ways."

I had thought of my abilities as convenient up to this point. Never as a weapon.

Our journey concluded at a space full of strange metallic structures. I stared, trying to make sense of what I saw. Miss approached the left side of a gold-colored structure, pulled it open, and looked at me like I should do the same on the right side. I did, and after watching her ease herself inside, I imitated her, which was easy to do since I had been dragging my legs behind me for minutes.

She chuckled and pushed a button on the dashboard. The machine roared to life.

"This is a transport?" I asked. "I have read about these."

"Yes. When I was your age, we called them cars until the recent invention of the fusion engine. Then, they became transports."

Once the thing started moving backward, I found myself clutching whatever I could grab. I had never ridden anything that moved. Miss steered it out of its space and into the world. We were traveling at a ridiculous speed. The distance we covered would take days on foot. Everything I saw around me was the historic holographic world I had studied brought to life—mountains, roads, transports, people with hair, music—oh the music! Melodious tones played in transport to a rhythm that bounced in my inner being. At a certain point, she rolled down the windows, and I craned my neck out into the wind. The icy, clean-smelling breeze initially felt like cold stabs on my skin. The pain was new and slightly pleasurable. When I had enough, I sat back.

"Amirah."

My manufactured name still did not sound like me. "Yes?"

"My name is Sasha."

Sasha. "Will anyone else be eating with us, Miss Sasha?"

"My husband—he insisted on meeting you—and our guest, Natalee."

Natalee. I practiced mouthing her name, as forenames were new to me. Was Natalee a girl or *the* girl—the one I needed to eliminate?

Whatever we ate was of little consequence to me. More of interest to me was whether or not Natalee was the right girl. To determine that was my primary objective for this entire night. So, Sasha was correct. While I did not plan to kill Natalee or anyone tonight, should my powers return to full strength, I intended to do so. "Are you...like me?"

"In a way."

The responses came from the back of the transport. I turned around and saw three women identical to Sasha. She could clone herself. I blinked, and the women disappeared. "Your husband, he..."

"Flight, superhuman strength, invulnerability."

This was the reason he wanted to meet me—to protect his wife. "And Natalee?"

"She does not have abilities."

My shoulders sagged, I hoped, outside of her peripheral vision. The progenitor of the nuclear winter must not be that close to her after all.

We stopped in front of a structure that looked large enough to fit both the Hub and my compound inside of it. Lit up at the front, the bottom, and the top, the front appeared to be built from stone and wood. More than anything, I wanted to go inside and experience the luxuries I had only heard, read, or viewed about. Again, I mimicked the manner in which Miss...*Sasha*...moved. I swung my legs out first, sighed, and pushed my body forward, shutting the door behind me. It occurred to me she might have a back injury, and I decided I should move more naturally.

Though the home's decor piqued my interest in every way, I played down my enthusiasm. A stationary living structure made of brick, wood, and gypsum—it was a myth come to life! My feet hurt, so when Sasha took off her shoes at the entrance, I did the same, and my feet expressed gratitude. She pointed to a piece of furniture that resembled the one Nine and Thirteen had allowed me to sleep on, but its cushions were plush and appeared to be softer. "Please, have a seat. I need to use the restroom. I'll be right back. Stay here."

I did as she said, and she disappeared. *Indoor plumbing.* I had no pressure on my bladder or bowels, but I wanted to try it. Maybe the mechanisms were similar to that of Nine and Thirteen's place.

Immediately in front of me was a large gray orb. Holovision had been invented but not perfected to the level I had been accustomed to yet.

"Holovision on," I called out. The machine flickered on and played far softer than I had anticipated. While the live stream's host spoke about the nuclear explosion on United States soil in December 2029, I read the crawling print at the projection's bottom: WORLDWIDE PANIC, GEOPOLITICAL CONFLICT: Search for answers extends to miles-wide radius of ground zero.

A smaller place similarly designed to the building we had left, what the woman on the program called a private industrial complex, had been seized by government agencies with unfamiliar acronyms as they did not exist in my time.

This was the beginning of the end. Whoever started this nuclear winter was, they had to be stopped.

The temperature in the air became intolerable. Never had I been this hot. My skin wasted no time producing sweat. I looked away from the holovision and saw a brown-skinned girl leaning over the staircase and staring at me. Dark yellow smoke emanated from beneath her eyelids. The intangible hatred and intense rage from this person... She wanted to destroy me.

It was *her*.

The Nuclear Winter.

It had to be.

This was my shot.

Her glowing eyes hissed and spat scalding blasts at me. For my entire life until I arrived in 2029, besides me, I knew of Almunashiy and Nazirah having abilities. In a matter of weeks, I had met Sasha and this girl. How were powers more common now? Were they genetically bred, like mine, mutations, or something else?

I dove forward in the direction of the holovision projector, and she incinerated the furniture I had been sitting on instead.

I held my hand up and shouted, "Wait!"

She shot at me again. Pinned between the holovision projector and an inferno, I had no other choice than to attempt to use my powers as a shield. Needles jabbed through my head when I projected the portal, but it swallowed everything she threw in my direction and sent it to the Narrow Space. She would have incinerated me if the bracelet had completely nullified my powers. And what of hers? If these were her tempered powers, then she could decimate Earth with ease.

"Natalee!" Sasha screamed and extinguished the fires with a device that shot white foam. "Stop!"

"I can't!" she cried.

Natalee? The one without powers? Miss Sasha had lied to ambush me!

Blood cascaded from my nose. I closed my mouth to avoid swallowing it, and it washed down my chin and stained my shirt and the front of my pants. Letting down my shield meant being vaporized, so I could not do it no matter the cost.

The heat dialed down, and the attack stopped. Besides the crackling embers surrounding me, the only other sounds were that of our panting breaths. Natalee slumped against the wall. Miss Sasha leaned over, hands on her knees. While I had stopped hemorrhaging, my clothes were soaked with blood. I did not have the strength to move.

In front of me was another girl—a *different* girl—her face downcast with sorrowful eyes.

190

FIFTEEN

The one called Natalee did not stop attacking me on her own. She stopped shooting her destructive eye beams the instant this brown-haired girl jumped between us. A human shield—like Almunashiy had done for me. I owed my life to someone again, once to Almunashiy and now to this stranger. Without reliable passage back to my reality, my one way to honor her was by doing what she had sacrificed for me to accomplish—murder the Nuclear Winter.

"Move out of the way, Lucy!" Natalee screeched and waved.

"Take the shot!" Lucy coughed. The black smoke and fumes overwhelmed them but not me as they were no worse than the normal, everyday air in 215 that irritated my lungs.

"You're in my shot. I'll take you out, too."

"I said take the shot! Do it!"

I had been mistaken. The objective of this human shield was not my protection. *She wanted to go with me.*

Natalee scrambled down the stairs and approached us, which forced the girl closer to me until we were near enough to embrace. At this distance, she would certainly die. She was young, diminutive, and wiry limbed, more so than me. Natalee could not have done damage to me without seriously harming her friend as well, but she did not try. Her pupils sizzled and flickered bright orange but they did not strike again.

Out of breath, Miss Sasha finally entered the room wearing a padded black vest covering her from the neck to the waist. Keeping a careful distance, she surveyed the smoldering damage to the furniture and walls. I did not understand why she did not help guard me until I viewed her hands resting atop her belly. While there was no bulge, I had to assume she was with child. Were Natalee's energy to have a high enough level of radioactivity, it would destroy Sasha's child. The distance and protective vest now made sense.

My smartwatch measured the home's radioactivity at barely under 100 rads. A bit higher and all of us, except maybe the person emitting the radioactivity, would be dead.

Frantic, Natalee yelled over our shoulders. "Call him, Sasha! She'll kill Lucy. It's what she came here to do."

"No!" Lucy screamed. "I want to hear from her why she's here!"

Sasha coughed and twisted a black ring on her left ring finger until it glowed red. "Let *him* ask her, Lucy! Back away!"

"My grief is not a blindfold." She sharply inhaled before continuing. "And I'm not an idiot! You want to know everything, too, if she's like the Forecaster, to see what she knows. That's why you studied her for all this time, right? Why you brought her here?"

The accusation made sense. Finally, I understood all of the motivation behind keeping me alive and bringing me here. They were altruistic from a certain point of view. I had arrived from the future with helpful information for avoiding a catastrophic reality. Anything I said could knit a thread in the timeline and lead straight to the hellscape I had been sent to help avoid. I had been told the one thing to do to avoid it was to kill the girl who initiated the nuclear winter. All else would not do.

But was that the truth? Who or what determined the ways the timeline flowed? Those who could alter it, like me? A divine being? Time and chance?

Nothing?

"Lucy—"

"Call off the beacon, Sasha! He won't understand!"

The mother-to-be violently shook her head. "You don't know what she'll do."

"Call it off! You know what he'll do once he sees her!" Her hot breath tickling the hair inside my nose, Lucy said, "You look like the others who came for me. Why? Why me?"

"How long..." I rushed the question out of my mouth. I must understand the terms of my death sentence. Swallowing hard, I added "...do I have to answer?"

"He won't go supersonic in this airspace but not long. Answer fast."

My chest burned. My impending death approached. "I am not like them, the others."

"Liar!" Natalee shouted curses at my face.

Lucy instructed her to stand down, and, for whatever reason, she obeyed. "You look like them," she said.

"I am not one of them."

Sasha's husband was coming. How long did I really have—seconds? Beneath their yelling, I listened for a change, *any change,* in the home environment for my executioner's approach. Sasha had not said he could turn invisible, but she had not disclosed Natalee's burning eyeballs either. Would he murder through stealth, or would the instruments of my death be blunt, heavy, forceful?

"Are you here to kill me then?" she asked.

A hard lump formed in my throat. I nodded. "If you are the bringer of the nuclear winter. It's what I was told to do."

"Told to do by whom?"

"It is why Almunashiy sent me…to save my world."

"Then you *are* like the others. And save your world from what?" she asked. My predecessors must have kept their interactions limited to non-conversational assassination attempts. She truly did not know. How could I tell her?

It turned out I did not have to. Her face muscles drooped. "Oh," she flatly said. *"Me."*

Lucy's tone was accepting. With no resistance or fight from her, how had my doppelgᴜnger failed to eliminate her? I did not understand. "You are the harbinger of the nuclear winter then?"

She bowed her head. "I guess I am. Will I feel it? I don't want to feel anything."

How does one describe death? I whispered, "I do not know. I have not—"

"Well, get on with it, then. My father is coming, and he will not hesitate to stop you."

The despair in her expressions suddenly made sense.

Urging my fingers into a fist, I called upon my power to summon a portal. My eyes met Lucy's. "Do not inhale before you walk inside. You should pass out before feeling too much."

Tears dropped from her face onto my blood-drenched shirt. "Okay," she muttered.

I had felt that way before, compelled to swallow poison, stay out in 215's atmosphere until it overcame me, or breathe in the Narrow Place. Rather than feel hatred toward her for what she had wittingly or unwittingly done to me and the fabric of my former reality, my heart hurt with compassion.

She was much younger than me. I did not sense malice in her at all, and wishing for death forced me to reconsider my actions. Perhaps, instead of ill intent, she courted chaos, like Natalee, when employing the fire in her body.

For me to mete justice to a person with full knowledge of their behavior seemed different than a lawless being without the tools to govern themselves. Lucy might as well have been an infant stumbling onto Ordnance. Sasha was right. There was another way. Lucy eyed the bracelet Sasha had given me and used her own fiery vision to disable it. Once freed, my portal opened large enough for her to fit comfortably inside.

With little else to lose, I walked in after her and closed the wormhole behind me. Natalee dare not attack me and lose her friend forever. She and Sasha helplessly watched. Lucy had done what I said, and from the redness in her eyes and the flush of her tanned skin, she would soon be unconscious.

My doppelgänger was wrong. *She* had failed. I had not.

All I had to do was open another wormhole to escape and leave her to die.

Leave her to die or create another reality. Should I choose the latter, when? With no guarantee the strain would not trigger a crippling brain bleed, I could not go far. Acting on instinct alone, I generated an exit. Inside, I warned myself not to look back.

Wracked with guilt over murder by omission, I dragged her through with me.

We emerged across the way from her home. From the sun's overhead position and the crisp, dead leaves under my suddenly cold feet, it was midday during the fall or winter season. Besides swallowing a soft, metallic tasting mass large enough to choke on, which I assumed to be a blood clot, I felt normal but exhausted.

Once she revived, Lucy rushed me behind a tree. Meanwhile, a gathering of people dressed in black clothing had approached the front of her home. Looking down at my own garb, I saw the cause for concern.

She seemed preoccupied by something else. "Why didn't you just do us all a favor and *end* me?"

Struggling to explain the act of mercy to her, for I did not quite understand sparing the person who had destroyed my reality, I stuttered. "I-I..."

"And how did you choose *this day* of all days to time travel to?" She closed her right hand near her temple and opened it.

We had skipped through time, too? What had I done?

"I guess just poof! It popped in your head?"

The words sounded sincere. Her tone did not. "I did not focus."

"Didn't focus?" She hissed the S in focus. "Well, focus and get me out of here. You could not have chosen a worst day."

"I cannot." Thinking past the throbbing in my skull was impossible. "I need a moment."

She scowled. "Why do you always talk in complete sentences? Are there no contractions, curses, or slang words wherever you are from?"

The travel had caught up to my brain. "What day is this?"

Lucy drew a sharp breath. "December 11, 2029."

"How do you know?"

"Because I know," she shot back. "And if we are stuck here for any length of time, you will need clothes that don't make you look like a walking corpse. Wait here."

I watched her as she jogged up to the front door and opened it. She favored her left leg. She must be injured. From the voice's pitch, whomever had greeted her did so with surprise. I realized we had failed to eliminate this reality's version of Lucy, the 2029 Lucy, and should they have encountered one another, the effects could be far-reaching.

Before anything further happened, my smartwatch adjusted itself. Indeed, it was December 11, 2029 at 12:12 p.m."

Either the other version of her needed to be eliminated, or we would have to do as she suggested and leave this reality. Prior to doing so, I needed to replenish my strength and allow my brain to heal.

Moments later, I noticed a window opening on the home's second story. Lucy crawled through the window onto the roof and closed it. Once she had sufficiently checked for onlookers and secured the bag on her back, she leaped to an adjacent tree and climbed down the trunk.

Breathless, she limped over and handed me the clothes. "Here," she gasped. "These are the baggiest things I own. You look about the same size in the shoes. Try them on."

"Here?"

She raised her eyebrows. "You can't go inside the house. Anywhere else besides here will draw more attention. Hurry!"

The brisk fall air helped motivate me to quickly strip and redress. Inside the bag was a white undershirt, a black, thick hooded sweatshirt and sweatpants as she called them, and dark gray and white shoes that perfectly fit.

"What is this multicolored winged animal on my chest?"

"A *mariposa*—a butterfly. It's an insect. Rhapsody used to call me—you've never seen a butterfly before? Aren't there insects in the future?"

"We have flies, ants, and roaches, not much else."

After I wiped my bloodied chest down with the old clothes, she tossed them into a tall green garbage receptacle left in the street. The pain in my head had lessened but not completely subsided.

"Once we eat, you'll take us back," she said with certainty.

I followed her down the walkway. "I will not exist for almost forty years from this point in time, but we cannot run into you—the 2029 you from this reality."

"Why not?" she asked. "It'd be cool to meet my past self."

"Temporal displacement, temporal paradox..."

She stopped walking. "Temporal *what* now?"

Without my nootropics, I lost much of the vocabulary and information I attained beneath Vagrant City, so I used my palm to illustrate. "From what I remember of quantum many worlds interpretation, and it is not much—"

"Many worlds? Like more than this one exist?"

"Almunashiy warned me about two versions of one person existing in one reality." I drew a letter X across my palm's breadth with my left forefinger. "One must erase the other."

We resumed our walk. "So, how do twins exist in one reality?" she asked.

"Identical twins are not the same," I told her. "Different experiences and histories—you and your past self cannot be in the same place at the same time."

"So, erase her. And by erase, you mean..." She pantomimed a stabbing to the heart with an imaginary blade. Once I affirmed this, she said, "Lovely. Well, does whomever does the erasing matter?"

I shrugged.

"You erased the version of you who tried to kill me?"

"No," I told her. "She succumbed to injuries."

Her eyebrows raised at the news. "Pity. Well, today, I go to Xobai Beach, which is not close, so evading myself shouldn't be too hard for an hour or so. Let's go."

Near the end of the roadway, I bent over and gasped for air. When I exhaled, I saw my breath. At times, when the temperature at home plunged, we holed up inside our compounds for warmth when we had fuel. What other recourse did we have? Our threadbare clothes could not protect us against the elements like Lucy's wares did, especially the *mariposa* sweater. While I had to rub my hands to regain feeling, the rest of my body was warm.

I gained my bearings and caught up to Lucy. She had turned left and was halfway down the next walkway.

"Just up ahead," she said, pointing to a redbrick building.

The closer we came, the more aromas I detected; some kind of food, I supposed. My stomach growled with anticipation the closer we came to it. As we stepped inside, I witnessed the customs and imitated them once we sat. Lucy ordered two of everything she selected. I read the words on the rigid menu placard: raisin toast, scattered hash browns, cheese grits, eggs, and coffee. Whatever she had ordered, I would devour.

"Something my father taught me is because of who we are and what we do we must eat, so we might as well enjoy it and one another's company."

I fingered the edges of the silver utensils wrapped in paper. "I do not enjoy food."

"Why not?"

Meals in my reality were made to satisfy basic needs. We focused on survival. Lucy and the people she ate with, however, engaged in conversation about themselves and their daily lives—something she now expected me to participate in doing. Another old custom I must force myself to do. She had brought me clothes and food. I supposed I owed her the courtesy of conversation in addition to repaying my life debt.

Lucy sipped a dark-brown liquid she had made lighter with milk and a grainy substance she called sugar. I did the same, and as the pleasant, sweet bitterness slid down my throat, I posed the question at the forefront of my mind. "Why did you protect me from Natalee at your house?"

She set her cup down on the table as if my words had injured her. "I was not protecting you. But I'm not a murderer."

SIXTEEN

L ucy claimed she was not a murderer, but future history reframed her as one. In a matter of years, she would have the blood of billions on her hands. Using my smartwatch, I discreetly showed her holographic visuals of my home, what was left of it, and her jaw dropped.

"No. How could *I* do *that?*" she asked. "I'm not a…murderer."

She contested that her power scale, in her most destructive display, destroyed a building and caused a substantial weather disturbance over a small landmass. The one bit of proof to the contrary I could offer her was how our record coincided with the exact date of her display and how four more powerful occurrences happened over the years.

"The serum," she muttered. "Since that night, I've struggled with control...switching my powers on and off. The longer I don't use them, the more my bone cancer comes back. The sicker I become. I use them a little. No place anyone would notice."

Life in a world with ongoing radiation swells had taught me about cancerous cells and what they could accomplish in a human body. "Your abilities keep the disease at bay?"

"Yes."

"Unusual. The same with your friend Natalee?"

"She got a transfusion of my blood. None of us knew she had my powers until you showed up on my doorstep today...or whenever you arrived. A month from now? God, how do you keep all of this straight?"

I hadn't had to until recently. "And your leg?"

Lucy cursed and said, "I was shot last week...whenever, the first week of December 2029. Super healing has not kicked in yet."

Our food arrived. Thereafter, we ate in silence. The gelatinous texture of the yellow eggs on my tongue turned my stomach, yet I chewed and swallowed everything on my plate, even the leavened bread and crisp carnivorous by-products, and I drank multiple cups of coffee.

At the meal's end, though I had some energy again, weariness settled in my limbs. Digestion would take a while. My mind, however, was clear and pain free, which was a welcome change.

Once Lucy wiped her face with a white paper and handed payment to the man who had brought our food, we departed. She suggested an oft-neglected cemetery behind a church for our trip. Her rationale for doing so was lack of surveillance, and we were less likely to be seen stepping through an interdimensional portal.

Returning to when we left would mean life to her and death to me. Sasha had refused to silence the beacon for her husband, and from what they said, he was not a man given to reason. I spared his daughter. Why was I not worth sparing?

Then, I decided not to take her back to that reality.

In a way, my resolution to do the best for myself felt wrong, rebellious. Never in my life had I experienced such a strong self-preservatory urge, but it thrilled me. My heart leaped. I did not want to die, and for once, the desire to live was not linked to Almunashiy or anyone else besides myself. Lucy could make her desires known or threaten to destroy me; however, nothing could leverage me into doing her bidding against my will. I readied myself for her request to return and rehearsed how I would say no.

We stood in front of a granite and limestone grave marker which read *Ruby Martinez, beloved mother, grandmother, and friend.* Lucy said, "Remember at the diner when I told you that I'm not a murderer, Amirah?"

"I do."

Lucy stared at a clump of brown grass near her shoe edges. That's not exactly true."

Her statement immediately put me on the defensive. Keeping my eyes on her as I backed away, I thought about teleporting anyplace where she could not find me.

Palms out in a surrender motion, she confessed, "I thought you deserved the truth. Or maybe I needed to say it out loud. Today's the wake. A wake is a ceremony"— Lucy choked on her own sobs but continued—"-where you say nice things...about the dead person...you vaporized... It wasn't my fault. I didn't mean to kill her!"

"Who?"

Her lips puckered inward, and she whispered, "Rhapsody Lowe...*my mom.* On my fifteenth birthday. December 4, 2029."

The date struck a chord in my chest. Her birthday, her mother's death, was the precursor to my world's history.

I considered Almunashiy to be like a mother to me since I did not have birth parents. I understood this pain more than she knew. Though I had not taken

Almunashiy's life, her sacrifice, like Rhapsody's, I imagined, helped me feel complicit in her demise. Therefore, a small part of me felt compelled to help prevent it from happening.

"This guy injected me with a drug...my powers spiked...burned so much...I couldn't handle it," Lucy explained through hitching breaths and wild tears. "The surge...Rhapsody...my mom flew me into the atmosphere...my energy...and she died...because of *me*. West Virginia isn't a smoldering crater of skeletons because of her.

"I am sorry for your loss."

Lucy took my hands. Her cold fingers were dry and rough. "*This* is why you saved me. Save her *and* your world."

How could I do both? I withdrew my hands and told her no. "I saved you because it was the humane thing to do, what Almunashiy would have wanted, what she died for."

Lucy retrieved a device from her pocket and swiped her fingers across its illuminated glass face. "What is that A word you keep saying?"

I repeated Almunashiy and spelled it for her. "It is Arabic."

She read her device's display. "For creator. Is that why you are so devoted to her? It's your name for God or a god?"

Her face appeared in my mind's eye. "Humans from my time are cultured from cells, so she created me. She was both a mother and father to me, and I-I will never see her again. I have accepted that."

My voice wavered as I spoke. There was a sadness inside my words I previously did not know ran so deep. Lucy wondered aloud if I could go back to my point of origin, forget about everything, and be with the woman I loved. While possible, I weighed whether certain death with Almunashiy exceeded the survivability of our plan.

"Don't you see?" Her watery eyes lit up. "You don't *have* to accept that. You can travel to anywhere in the timeline you want. Go—"

"No, I—"

"Go back a week and prevent the explosion. Put the guy who injected me in that dark place we were—"

"the Narrow Space."

"Put him in the Narrow Space, and past me will never detonate. Your reality, and mine, will change for the better. So, okay, maybe you can't go back to, I can't pronounce that A word...your mother, but you can go forward and still live a good life, maybe even find this reality's version of her."

From a certain vantage point, the plan was sound. On its face, preventing her from receiving the drug would restore her control. She and her mother would live, and my future was in the past no matter what I did. Spending the remainder of my life in a lush, intact world would have to suffice. Finding Almunashiy here was hopeless.

"Seven days?" I asked her.

"Better make it eight...December third. That way, there's margin for error. I'll go with and be your backup."

Lucy gave me coordinates and told me we would exit outside of the compound where Sasha had detained me. "Two versions of you cannot exist in one reality. You cannot hesitate."

She rolled her eyes. "I know, I know. I've got it under control."

I marveled at the jagged rock formations towering around us. A mighty wind gust blew. Lucy reached for me and grabbed me by the *mariposa* on the sweatshirt. She had known to brace herself to keep her balance. Startled and exhausted from leaping through realities, I sank to my knees. With my weight dead on the surface, my chances at staying on the cliff were better. Plus, with my eyes closed, the nausea waves slowed.

Lucy screeched, "What is the time here? I need to know when we are?"

I belched, and a small amount of food rushed into my throat that I spat out. My long answer was finding a source by which to calibrate my smartwatch. Outside, given I was on the northern hemisphere, and I could see the sun, I could wager a decent guess. But Sasha had adjusted my tech to technology available in 2029, so I checked. "One minute past ten hundred—ten p.m. on December third," I mumbled. With the full white moon in the sky, the time explained the horizon's dark-blue horizon, the black shadows covering us, and the air's temperature.

Lucy crouched next to me. "My parents were here, close by, which means I am asleep." She pointed behind us. "The compound is that way. We'll have to climb a bit."

The path was daunting, especially with only the moonlight and the illumination from our wrist devices to light the way, but once we got past the most treacherous parts, there was a path. Mere feet from the entrance, a small orb with a blinking red light scanned Lucy's face. "Identified: Luciana Debra Sandoval," said an automated voice.

My falsified identity had been constructed to pass muster in 2084, not 2029. Clearly, her part of the plan had flaws in it from the start. I had been naive, and my naivete would cost me. When it was my turn, the laser scan failed after two tries, and the voice demanded I identify myself. "Amirah..." I paused, almost forgetting my manufactured surname. "Mostafa. Amirah Mostafa."

"Zhang!" Lucy shouted at the orb. "Let me in!"

"Lucy?" a man asked. "I thought you were asleep in your mom's quarters."

Hand on her hip, she shot back, "Couldn't sleep. Needed a walk. I'm excited for my birthday tomorrow. You get it, right?"

"Who is that with you? She's not in the facial recognition database or in uniform."

"That's 'cause she's new."

"There's no Amirah Mostafa I see on the planet. What is *really* going on?"

"I'm Lucy from a month in the future."

I almost cursed her myself. Now, there was no way we would get inside. Had she given any thought to how to negotiate us inside before this moment?

Lucy cursed and talked to me out of the corner of her mouth. "Can you teleport us behind this door?"

My stomach clenched. "Without seeing where I'm going? We could end up anywhere."

"Stop looking at me like that. You've been in here before. Think of a spot, and take us there."

"Lucy..."

"Hurry!"

The doors opened, and I caught a glimpse of weapon-bearing men before I transported us to somewhere inside of the complex I recognized from the future. "Go!" she shouted. "Go someplace and hide, and I'll find you."

Without time to consider what was happening to me, I pulled the sweatshirt's hood over my head and quickly walked like I had a destination to reach. Nobody stopped me or gave me a second glance that I noticed. Orbs like the one at the entrance we had breached lined the ceilings at the hallway intersections. Each time I passed one, they prompted me to stand still for identification purposes. When I ignored them, they buzzed and issued an ominous warning. "Intruder alert! Intruder alert!"

Somehow, I reached the shower suite. Ducking in, I stripped out of the clothes Lucy had given me and rummaged through the storage locker for clothes my size. After several attempts, I discovered a set that looked as if it would fit me—first pants then a shirt and shoes. I sent the discarded clothes into the Narrow Space to avoid detection. Nearby, I saw a row of crude-looking circular disks that, from first glance, appeared to be similar to the bodysuit I had been outfitted with in Vagrant City. I placed it at the base of my neck and was pleasantly surprised when flexible body armor crawled across my body and formed a mask.

Now, I could move around in true anonymity.

Three women in black uniforms and armed with heavy Ordnance entered the area. I ducked behind a wall, thought of the first place in the complex I could clearly remember—my old room—and exited a wormhole there. I was at the foot of the bed, which was occupied by Lucy. She was wearing different clothes, and the room was sweltering. According to the heads-up display, the room's temperature was one hundred and thirty-six degrees. To the right of the bed was a pile of gray ash with white shards in it. She had eliminated the possibility of temporal displacement.

I smiled and dropped my mask. "You did it!" I said. "What do we do next?"

Lucy raised her hands. Orange flames rippled around her fingers.

SEVENTEEN

The young woman in front of me was not the Lucy I had brought from 2030. That Lucy, 2030 Lucy, was perpetually on the verge of shedding tears. This Lucy had trembling lips and darting eyes. Moments before I arrived, without context, she had committed murder against herself. Whatever I told her next must ground her after her actions had cast her adrift. "I will not hurt you." I spoke in the gentlest tone I could muster. "My name is Amirah."

She kept up her guard. Her eyes darted to the ash. "Who are you, and who was that?"

"There is no easy answer—"

"Who was it? A shapeshifter like Kendel?"

Shapeshifters existed? Those who could alter their form? I did not know how that could be surprising given all I had recently experienced. "That was a version of you from the future."

Lucy rapidly blinked. "What? That's what she said. That's impossible. You're both lying."

A quick movement might come off as threatening. Instead, I moved with careful purpose. "No, I am not. She knew where to find you and how to get you to kill her."

Her hands returned to normal. "I...she...didn't even fight back. Why?"

In a way, I did not blame her for defending herself against what she perceived was a threat. However, the fact she had leveled another human being to ash we were presently inhaling raised the hair on the back of my neck.

"Two of you cannot exist simultaneously," I said without going into gross detail, "and I think that she did not want to be here anymore."

There were no more follow-up questions regarding her doppelgänger's death. With less than a week's difference between her then and now, the same struggles, thoughts, and feelings were at work in her mind. Her mother Rhapsody's death was probably not the lone reason for her despair, but whereas she had lived with her grief in my original reality, in this new one, she had succumbed to it. "You can time travel?" she asked.

"Yes."

"Then I should not do to you what I did to her."

The Lucy from 2030 had told me she was not a murderer, but *this* Lucy had promptly destroyed herself. Had she paused to ask herself anything, question anything? Did they have a conversation like we were doing now? What were her final words? Did she have anything to say? Or had the Lucy I knew given into despair and pressed her body against the flaming hands?

And now, this Lucy threatened my life. I could easily escape. Did she know this? Thus far, I had not shown aggression toward her. I could shove her into a black hole and the pressure would crush her lungs and blood vessels. Surely, I received credit for the reticence and self-restraint not to do so.

We were both dangerous. One of us had to make the first move.

Her brow furrowed, and the flames lost some of their color and vibrancy. "Why would future me want to die on purpose now? I'm the happiest I've ever been. What will happen to me in a week to change that?"

"I mean you no harm, Lucy. None of it has to happen—"

"Tell me!"

Sweat beaded on my forehead as the room temperature skyrocketed. "Tomorrow, Rhapsody will die."

Those four words extinguished her flaming hands. "On my birthday? No," she mumbled. "How?"

"It does not matter," I said. Nothing about Lucy's mental stability suggested she could handle the truth. "She will live depending on the steps we take from here."

"Why should I trust you? Who's to say you don't kill my mother?"

A valid question. "You'll have to trust me, *mariposa*."

Lucy's skin flushed, and her eyes fluttered. "Who told you my mother called me that?"

"You did."

From there, she was willing to listen. I spelled out everything I could remember that 2030 Lucy had said to me, from being injected with a serum causing her to lose control of her powers to the inevitable explosion that would claim Rhapsody's life.

"And the explosion I cause...I'm the one responsible for her death?"

Hers and so many others. "Your abilities grow beyond your ability to restrain them."

"But, it's *me*. It's me. That guy was right. I am the Nuclear Winter. I *will* destroy the planet."

She glanced down at the gray dust and blackened bones and sobbed. To help ease the pain, I sent 2030 Lucy's remains through a portal. Her wails eventually waned into quiet whimpers. "His name is Liam. If he will trick my parents and attack this place to get to me, the easiest solution is to kill me and go back to your reality. I'm dying of cancer anyway."

I explained to her that overusing my abilities would cause my brain to stroke out. "There is no going back," I said.

Lucy crossed her arms and sucked her teeth. After a moment or two, she tapped the inside of her ear. "Zhang," she said. "Come to my mother's room, please."

Instantly, a slender man with spiky hair appeared in a wispy cloud of terrible-smelling green smoke. In one deft movement, he placed a bracelet on my left wrist like the one Sasha had given me. "Good job," he said. He touched his ear the same way Lucy had. "We discovered the intruder in the barracks sector. Standby for transport to detention level."

Lucy grabbed Zhang's arm and said, "Wait, no! I called you to help, not capture her!"

"You don't understand," he responded. "Liam will infiltrate this facility however he can, including sending a spy—"

"A spy? You don't get it! She called me a nickname nobody knows but my mom, and I think she's the key to stopping Liam."

"Maybe, maybe not," he said. "We'll find out."

Before I could react to the betrayal, Zhang teleported me into a room with dark-gray walls and no way to see in or out. I waved my hand in front of my face until the pungent green cloud subsided. Best as I could surmise from my surroundings, I had been taken prisoner alone. That was until I heard the echo of nonsensical words coming from the inside of the wall farthest to my left. My energy sapped by the bracelet, I dragged myself toward the sounds. The closer I came, the less sense they made. Pounding on the wall with my fists, I called out, "Hello? Is there anybody there?"

"Die!" a female babbled.

Zhang materialized at the room's center as a 3D hologram. "That will do you no good. The Forecaster will not respond to you."

The Forecaster. The one with abilities similar to mine except she could open wormholes and predict the future while I could only travel to it. "Let me go!" I shouted.

"Who are you *really?*" he asked me.

He was not ready for the truth, but I relented. "My name is 1-13-9-18-1-8."

Zhang typed the number in on a display. "You are missing a digit of your social security number. What is it?"

I did not understand. "Why does everyone keep saying that? Not one hundred thirteen, 1-13-9-18-1-8 is what I am called in 2084. We do not use forenames and surnames as you do."

"You're from fifty-five years in the future," he said, stifling laughter. "Right. No first or last name... That's convenient. Who wins the 2030 NBA Finals so I can bet?"

His flippancy struck a nerve. "You, Sasha, Natalee, Lucy's father...everyone you care for on this planet will die if you do not listen to me and carefully do what I say."

Zhang's holographic lips puckered. "Is that a threat?"

"It is the future," I said. "You have not heard what Lucy will do tomorrow."

His eyes flashed up. I had gotten his attention. "Tomorrow," he repeated. "Tell me, Forecaster number two, what will happen tomorrow?"

I told him everything. Liam would turn their plan against them, invade and devastate this place, shoot a chemical into Lucy, which would make her explode, killing Rhapsody and setting her on the path the end the world with her chaotic gifts.

While I explained, Zhang's face was emotionless. To prove my point, I accessed the holographic displays of my home world. This, too, left little effect on him. Either he believed me and had no feelings toward it, or he thought everything I said was fiction.

At the end of my explanation, he asked, "Is there anything else I need to know?"

"No," I responded.

"Then, thank you. We have everything we need."

Convinced I had done a good thing, I smiled. "Release me, and I can help."

Zhang's hologram disappeared. Suddenly, I heard hissing. Trails of white gas shot out from the ceiling corners and opening vents in the floor. The stolen armor formed around my body and face, but its filtration system did nothing to prevent the poison from seeping through. *Hydrogen cyanide gas.* When the name popped up on the heads-up display, I remembered its history, and its primary use to execute criminals.

Criminals.

From any perspective, had I done wrong? I had told them the way to avoid destruction, and they would execute me for it. I squeezed my fists until my knuckles throbbed and shook, but no Omnikhron appeared. This bracelet was meant to keep me completely powerless. Banging the bracelet against the unforgiving floor did not work except to hurt my wrist. I cursed it and crawled to the furthest corner away from the vents. Almunashiy once spoke of my incredible power being beyond comprehension. Perhaps she spoke of the alternate reality version of myself who murdered without regret and not who I believed myself to be: a good person trying to do the right thing.

Whatever was certain to work, I needed to find it soon. My bones felt as if they were fighting against my muscles and vice versa. Struggling to breathe, clutching and slapping at my throat and chest, I coughed but could not catch air.

The burning in my brain, the desperate feeling right before losing consciousness...

This was it.

I had imagined my final moments more than once. I thought everyone in Sector 215 wished for a peaceful death—to die in one's sleep, heart stopping without notice, sudden unexpected loss of brain function, anything with the least amount of suffering since suffering was all we knew. Dying this way was poetic. For most of my wretched life, I had given little thought to how long I would survive, and after wanting to live, the opportunity to do so was being snatched away from me. The unbearable pressure behind my eyes—would they burst open or pop out from their sockets?

The other me had been correct all along about my failure, comprehensive as it was. She spoke with such confidence and conviction about my downfall like a foretelling.

It did not matter.

Nothing did.

The power of conscious thought beyond me, I lay on the floor and waited for death.

EIGHTEEN

O f all the apocryphal and extant text descriptions I had read about the afterlife, none of them matched my current surroundings. Instead of angelic choruses draped in white and surrounded by blinding light or eternal fire and tortured howls of the damned, there was stifling darkness. Except, unlike the Narrow Space, I could breathe in the void.

Could this be nirvana? Then elders and ancient gods should be surrounding me. This was something different. The readings inside my mask did not make any sense. No location registered, the oxygen levels were at zero, and my vital readings were perfect though, a moment ago, I had inhaled poison gas.

"Hello?" My lips and jaw moved, and my throat tensed like normal, but without making a noise. *Almunashiy? Lucy? Sasha?* Closing my eyes, I yelled their names as if that were the difference between going unheard.

This was not heaven, hell, or nirvana. The one light source in the darkness, my smartwatch display, showed the final time and date it had registered—midnight on December 4, 2029. Without calibration, the display should have proceeded forward in time unless it broke or time did not move forward here.

The last thing I remembered was lying in a cell waiting to succumb to death; however, at the moment, I did not feel pain. I possessed the ability to read, so I hypothesized I was not in a dream. This place had to be ruled by some sort of physical laws although there was no atmosphere, and yet, I could breathe. What was I inhaling and exhaling? Oxygen was the only substance a human could breathe to survive.

Or was it?

What else might I be able to do here?

With the bracelet restraint still on my wrist, I had a fleeting thought about removing it. Suddenly, my arm from fingertip to elbow, including my smartwatch, vanished. Panicked, I wished my limb to return, and it rematerialized intact without the bracelet. The disappearing sensation was strange, not painful, akin to being submerged in water—weightless and numb, nonexistent.

Fear of permanent intangibility and invisibility gripped my heart each time a body part left me, but, as I could go forward or backward in time at will and this place did not harm me, I continued practicing. To avoid losing balance and falling, I sat before trying to use this new ability on my legs, and I wondered what the surface I was sitting on was.

Before long, I had mastered making everything but my head disappear. This power was different than phasing in and out of alternate realities, but the one commonality was I had to think in order to control it. Who knew if I could not will my head back into existence with an intangible, invisible mind?

How long had I been here? There was no way to tell. I did not experience hunger, thirst, fatigue, or the sensation to relieve myself. My brain seemed intact. Assuming time did not pass here and this was a fixed point, I could go anywhere I wanted, and without bodily needs, there was no rush to choose. When I conjured an Omnikhron, my mouth gaped at the rotating blue gate's massive size, the largest I had ever seen. Five people, shoulder to shoulder, could have walked through it.

That was when the realization struck me.

This was the Narrow Space. Its nature had shifted, and the wormhole had not expanded, but *I* had. How any of this had happened, I was not sure. This changed everything for me. Lucy could safely detonate here without other casualties. Her mother would live. The world would survive.

I had not failed after all.

The stabbing sensation in my head was no more. Neither were the nosebleeds. I did not know why nor did I care. All that mattered was where to go next. Going back to the moment where and when I left, around midnight on December 4, 2029, meant dying in a gas chamber. I must go forward to complete my mission. Realigning my thoughts to an hour after I had departed the gas chamber, I reentered Lucy's room at one o'clock a.m. on December 4, 2029.

The Amirah from this 2029 had escaped a gas chamber, and I would not have to explain to this Lucy from hours later, who I was since we had already met two hours ago.

As soon as I appeared, Lucy, who had been sitting on the bed, shot a yellow energy stream at the room's top right corner. The surveillance camera melted and dropped to the floor in a black liquid heap.

This time, I was the one on guard and ready to strike.

"I'm so sorry, Amirah, I thought Zhang would help," she explained. "They are still looking for you."

Destroying the camera might have seemed like a good idea at the time to Lucy, but it would not be long until someone noticed. "We cannot stay here. I have an idea, but this time, you will have to trust me. Exhale all of the breath from your lungs."

I watched her chest deflate, and then, I opened a portal and reached out my hand, which she reluctantly took. On the other side, we emerged on the only other part of the building I knew besides the locker room and the place where I had previously stayed—the parking lot.

Lucy adjusted her voice to mute the echoes. "What time of day is it?"

I paused until my smartwatch adjusted. "December 4, 2029, evening, about twenty-one hundred hours. But, there's another you here, and—"

She took off running, and I followed. Wherever this reality's Lucy was, we needed to avoid her for now. I commanded my suit to cover my face. Once we reached the building's next level, I found keeping my identity hidden was the least of my worries. Masked people with Ordnance ran in the opposite direction. Hopefully, we would reach our destination soon. Burning pain flared on my right side, and though my head did not explode from hopping realities, I did not feel my best either. Doing another time jump would have to wait.

We stopped at a landing strip littered with winged transports. The ethereal blue glow in the open sky reminded me of that of an Omnikhron. A large air vehicle flew through it. Being told the future and seeing future events come to pass were two different things. My gut tensed. Lucy from 2030 had outlined the day's major events for me, but without specifics, I was guessing what happened and when. Soon, she would be confronted by Liam, and...

"Lucy!" A red-haired woman in body armor like mine grabbed her at the arms. "Where have you been? You missed training, your evaluation with Susan..." She tapped her ear. "I've located her, Director. Proceed full speed to rendezvous."

"Wait, no, Kendel!" she yelled. "It's a trap! Tell him to come back."

The light from the Omnikhron was gone. So was the Forecaster.

It was too late.

"Come back? Wh—"

Ordnance fire tore through the side of Kendel's face and exited through the other. Our masks formed around our faces too late to shield from the blood spray. The wet spatter covered our faces. They were shooting to kill, not to stun and capture.

Lucy focused her eyes on Kendel and the crimson pooling around her unmoving body. Someone stuck a hard surface into my back. What happened next both thrilled and amazed me. Ordnance shots painlessly blasted through my body. Looking down, I saw splashes of a viscous black liquid jump from my torso with each shot.

"That's interesting," said a man with an accent I had never heard before.

I did not turn around, but by the way Lucy's eyes widened, he must have retrained his weapon behind my back on her.

"Come with me, or she dies, and you will never see Natalee Gupta again."

This was the end. I could not have authored it better. Her blood would be on his hands and not mine. Natalee would not become the Nuclear Winter in her stead. Then, once I eliminated him, the future would be secure. "Then they die," I said, "but without Lucy, you can't activate the provenance crystal tonight. And her parents will not be gone long enough for you to try another way."

According to 2030 Lucy, in the original version of their story, Liam sided with a high-ranking government official, nearly killed her, and he escaped with fragments of whatever a provenance crystal was.

This Liam, who had just murdered the girl named Kendel, raised his hand, and the shooting from his underlings stopped until he fired three shots into Lucy.

The blunt thud sound sickened me. Lucy, at least the one I had brought here from December 3, was dead now, too. The one from this time, I'd call her *mariposa*, was at the bottom of the ravine.

"Kill this girl," he said to no one I could see.

I sent an Omnikhron below Liam's feet, and he dropped through it into the Narrow Space. I stepped through another portal and escaped to the canyon below. Here, if the story 2030 Lucy told me was true and the timing was right, I would find Lucy from this reality and, after eliminating her, finally rest.

A bright orange flare rocketed toward the fortress's platform. *Mariposa.* I had miscalculated. By the time I rejoined this Lucy on the launch stage, although her armor was shredded at the feet and many other places, she had taken out her assailants without incident. She would have remembered me as the girl who Zhang nearly executed, not the one who had told Liam to do his worst or the one who had sent Liam to a suffocating death. "You have to get out of here."

"No!" she shouted. "Nat is my best friend. I *have* to save her."

232

I hid the truth from her. "You are the key to it all," I responded. "You are the Nuclear Winter."

"Maybe," she admitted, "but *you* can bring my parents back."

"Not without knowing where they are, and I am not leaving y—"

Mariposa held up a finger to hush me. "Yeah. Yes, I'm here."

"Who is here?"

She held the finger to her mask. "I-It's secure. I'm Lucy...Champion. Lucy Champion...I'm fifteen...Philadelphia...December 4, 2014...I'm not alone. I have Amirah."

Unsure of whether or not to speak, I waited to hear the rest of the one-sided conversation. "I'll walk her through it, too."

According to this Lucy, Mariposa, once we accessed the back-channel section of our Wi-Fi connection, we could no longer be traced. Once we did so, I followed her through the dock walls after she blasted them to dust, circled around the northwest perimeter, and proceeded to the front corridor.

"What's next?" she asked to whomever was on the other side of the comm.

Until this moment, I had been following her in lockstep. A thought seized my limbs. *Everything the Lucy from 2030 had told me about today had come to pass. But had it happened because it was supposed to or because I had done nothing to change it? My mere presence and sending Liam to the Narrow Space should be enough to alter reality. What if it was not enough?*

A thunderous boom knocked me to the ground. A screeching, high-pitched tone hummed in my ears. The heads-up display diagnosed me with a Grade 3 concussion. The mask gave way, and I vomited onto a pile of debris. I swooned. The bright light pattern in my eyes kept me off balance.

I sat and closed my eyes, and when I opened them, she and I had been stripped of our armor and strapped down at the wrists, ankles, and waist on a bed. Through hazy vision—they must have drugged me while I was unconscious—I saw we faced a giant murky yellow gemstone. This was the provenance crystal Liam needed her to activate.

"When it's active," Mariposa said, "its wearer gains immortality and passive superhuman abilities. But it needs X-class solar flares or a radioactive charge to make it work."

A dose of Lucy's powers would reactivate it, and even though I had exiled Liam to the Narrow Space, history continued to repeat itself through someone else.

First, men dressed like the ones on the landing platform came to me. A golden-haired, pale-skinned woman, the one who appeared to be in charge, screamed curses at the man preparing to stick me with a silver needle. "Are you insane? Not *that* one!" she bellowed and pointed to Lucy. *"Her!"*

A man tied a small brown tube at Mariposa's right arm bend and injected her with a liquid I assumed would accelerate her powers.

NINETEEN

A ll that was left was getting her adrenaline to spike, to wit, the blonde woman—they referred to her as Becks—held what must be Ordnance in her right hand. With Liam gone, she must be planning to shoot Mariposa herself.

Silver firearm in hand, she pulled the trigger. A blast of bright orange light was accompanied by a boisterous explosion and spurts of blood. Lucy screamed and jerked against her bonds. In my peripheral vision, I noticed her eyes glowing like Natalee's had. She could not control it. Beams shot forth from her face, and as she glanced around, first up, then down, part of the ceiling and floor disintegrated and sizzled into hot clouds of dust. The resulting heat caused my entire body to perspire.

Soon, the men tilted her stretcher downward and pushed forward close enough so that she had no choice but to strike the provenance.

History was repeating itself.

Beneath my bonds, I squeezed my fist, and a portal opened between the beams and the stone. Becks shot both of my palms, and I yelled every obscenity I had ever heard. My throbbing bloody fingers broke my concentration and closed the portal. I could not think straight. Overhead, a rhythmic chopping sound echoed throughout the chamber.

"Becks!" one of the men yelled. "Time to go!"

Becks knelt close to the activated provenance and collected a handful of shards. From the way she winced and hurriedly placed them into a container on her hip, the things must have been hot. She was doing everything 2030 Lucy had told me Liam had done.

While Becks continued to sweep crystals into her hands, an almost naked Lucy freed me. I closed my eyes for fear her laser beams would melt my face off, but the nuclear radiance seemed to have spread throughout Mariposa's entire body. Despite the growing nuclear threat and impending destruction, her transformation was quite beautiful. I'd never seen light up close and personal like this before.

Becks fired once more at us. I cowered behind Mariposa. None of them hit me, and it did not appear that they struck her either. Without hesitation, Lucy's beams blasted Becks in the shoulder above the heart. I blinked and saw her no more. Had she vaporized her? A split second later, I sniffed a nauseating scent and witnessed a small puff of gold smoke where Becks had stood.

Ice-cold foam rained down on us. The heat from Lucy's powers dissipated. I stared down at my hands. Sure enough, the ammunition pellet had ripped through my palms and exited the back of my hand. The foam and bleeding gore kept me from seeing straight through them to the other side. I heard the click of metal against metal, two snaps, and another click. When I turned in its direction, I saw Becks had teleported back in front of us. Mariposa's eye blast had taken a good portion of her shoulder and some of her arm function.

She still fired at both of us, striking Mariposa in the chest and me in the arm and midsection. We collapsed onto the floor next to one another, dying.

Another Ordnance fired, electric-sounding, and sent Becks's firearm from her hand onto the floor. I spat out the blood pooling in my mouth. *Sasha.* Even looking sideways from the ground, I recognized her. Becks was beyond my line of sight, but she cursed Sasha for lasering two fingers off her hand before teleporting away.

238

Immediately, Sasha rushed over to us and gave us new bodysuit armor. Once it formed, it began diagnosing and treating my wounds, but what could it do for our internal bleeding?

"Who are you?" she asked me.

"A friend" was all I could manage to say.

Two armored people dropped through the ceiling and retracted their masks. From the man's severe-looking eyes and nose and the woman's brown hair and cheekbones, I assumed they were Lucy's parents—the mother who would give her life for her daughter and the father who, in 2030, had been called to eliminate me.

"You came," he said to Sasha.

"You called," she responded.

"Thank you," he said. Turning to me, he asked, "Who are you?"

Woozy from the blood loss, I lost my balance. Sasha sent a clone to my side to help steady me. "A friend," she said.

"From...the future," I added.

Everyone froze in place except Lucy who, from the way the temperature rose around us, was powering up again. "She..." I gasped and nodded at Lucy. "...will explode."

Sasha backed away, and said, "She's right. We have to get her as high as possible as fast as possible to minimize casualties before she detonates."

"Detonate? Like I'm going to explode? Won't that kill me?"

"Your power flushes out of you and replenishes itself, like a rechargeable battery. You'll probably absorb much of the gamma, neutron, and ionizing radiation you emit."

Yes, I thought. *And over the next fifty years or so, she will spew the energy out again and again and destroy the planet.* I moaned in dreadful pain.

Mariposa, her parents, and then Sasha looked at me to predict the outcome. When I did not answer, her father shot out. "Well? Will she survive?"

"Yes," I told them. After hissing my way through the increasing pain, I added, "but she will eventually kill everyone else on the planet."

"Everyone?" she mumbled. "Then you"—she winced—"all of you must get as far away from me as you can."

Her words sparked anger in me. "Nowhere is far..."The agony was too much for me to bear.

Their downcast faces said they believed I was telling the truth. "I'll stay with her," her father said. "I've been through this before. Remember the pit?"

"Not with this widened range of radioactivity, you haven't," Sasha said. "You'll die."

"Then, I die," he said.

Tears welled in Sasha's eyes.

"She's pregnant, Dad," said Mariposa. "Odds are, it's yours, right?"

Sasha openly sobbed, and Mariposa's father placed an arm around her shoulders. Rhapsody's head dropped.

"Mama," Mariposa said. Her powers surrounded her in an aura of orange light. "Help me!"

"Rhapsody!" Mariposa's father yelled. "No. Not both of you!"

As she fell to her knees, Rhapsody, joined her. "She's our daughter, Jason." She wrapped her arm around Lucy's waist and whispered something in her ear.

This was the end, where they would fly together into the ionosphere, Lucy would explode, Rhapsody would die, and the chain of events leading to a bleak future none of them could imagine would start.

Unless I did something.

Raising my right hand, I bent my fingers and sent Mariposa to the Narrow Space. When she fell through the portal into the void, Rhapsody tried to follow her, but I closed it too quickly.

"Send me after her!" she demanded. "Now!"

Mariposa's father, who Rhapsody called Jason, seethed and stood over me. He was not an exceptionally large man, but the threat of losing his daughter loomed, and I felt the anger building in him. "Where did you send her?"

Sasha spoke up. "It appeared to be some kind of black hole."

Rhapsody reached her hand *through me* and somehow touched my bleeding innards, which caused me to nearly black out with suffering. "Send me after her!"

I shook my head no even though she pulled at something painful inside of me. I blacked out for a moment, and when I awoke prostrate on the ground, Lucy lay next to me. Pale and motionless, she was no longer glowing. By her side, Rhapsody tried to resuscitate her.

"Back up!" Sasha said above Mariposa's mask. "Activate code AEG."

"Charging," said a mechanical voice. "Clear."

Mariposa's body spasmed with an electric shock. No one said anything besides Sasha. "Again," she commanded it.

"Charging," said the mechanical voice. "Clear."

I wanted to stay conscious long enough to witness Mariposa's death or which one of them would murder me for killing their daughter. My suit beeped with multiple

242

alerts about my blood loss, heart rate, blood pressure, and failing organs. That was until Rhapsody detached the probe from my neck and the suit retracted. Without its life-saving measures, I would die, too.

The last thing I saw was Mariposa's father lifting her limp form in his arms and carrying her to some undisclosed location. I blinked slowly until my eyes would no longer open.

I was no longer in pain.

Lying on my back, I was comforted by billowy softness I had not experienced before. I opened my eyes. The room was completely white. Machines to my right droned with measurements of my vital signs. According to the readings, I was indeed still on Earth and far from dead. My hands were healed with reddish-pink scars on both sides, and when I touched my midsection, I felt a rough lump from where the shot went in. The muscles in my arms were incredibly weak.

Someone knocked at the door before entering. I cleared my throat to speak, but nothing resembling sound came out. When they entered, I could not believe what I saw.

"Almunashiy?" I mouthed. My lips responded a second or two later than my brain had commanded them to.

"Good morning!" She even had her voice, albeit with a sharp accent and much happier than I had ever heard it. "What's that you said to me?"

I shook my head in frustration. She would not exist in the way I knew her. Here, somatic nuclear cloning might never become a reality. Was this truly her, the source DNA she came from, and not a doppelgänger? Only one way to tell? Forming my lips into noticeable words, I asked for her name.

"My name?" she repeated. "Eve."

"Adebisi?"

"Why, *yes,*" she responded. "How did you know?"

My eyes watered. This woman, named Eve, was indeed the source code for my mother figure—my mother. She had the forename and surname she had chosen for herself, too. "Are you from Africa, Eve?"

Eve nodded yes, raised her wrist, and spoke into her smartwatch. "Text Director Champion. She's awake."

It was not long before Lucy's parents showed up to the room. Neither of them seemed particularly happy to see me alive. I wondered if Lucy had survived, but I did not want to seem insensitive and be the first to mention it.

Lucy's father scratched his eyebrow with his pinky. I noticed the yellow wedding band on his ring finger. "We were wondering if you would wake up. You would have died from blood loss if Rhapsody had not removed the bullet from your spleen, and the doctors tending to you weren't exactly hopeful. You've been in a coma for six months."

Six months? "Lucy—"

"—is alive." Rhapsody's voice rang with gratitude. "So am I, thanks to you. That was risky, sending her to wherever, but her powers are under her control. Something to do with temporarily flat lining reset her adrenal gland, they said."

"Sasha's at home with our daughter, and Natalee sends her best."

Natalee, who had almost killed me, sent well wishes?

My heart swelled with emotion. "Window?" I whispered. Together, Jason and Rhapsody turned my bed and machines around to face the window behind me. He pushed the white curtains aside and pulled the shade. The morning sunlight blinded me at first. But, as my eyes adjusted to it, I noticed the clouds were white, not red, and no precipitation, purple or otherwise, fell from the blue sky.

It was a clear day. No threat of a Doomsday Clock. A new reality for me, and I was happy to get to see where it would go from here.

THE END

ACKNOWLEDGEMENTS

TO: My Lord and Savior Jesus Christ. Thank you for the ideas for a four (now six) book young adult science fiction series featuring the kind of children I teach every day (minus the super abilities).

My wife and business partner Heather and our three daughters. I could not have done this without you.

My parents, Bradley and Barbara, my stepmother, Debra, for her inspiration, and my editor on this project, Kelly Hartigan of Xterra Web.

A big thank you to those who advised me or inspired me regarding content and names: especially Claire Allen, Becki Brunette, Veronica Bridges, Alan Fowler, and Kendel McAuliffe.

Discover more by Brian Thompson

Eighth-grader Lucy Sandoval has no hope of reaching high school.

Blindsided by a terminal cancer diagnosis, she resolves to spend her last moments with the father she never knew. But he disappeared years ago, and Lucy's mother is tight-lipped about him and their shared past.

With little to no leads, Lucy's faith wanes further when their cross-country flight detonates mid-air and they survive.

Following a firefight with a group of mercenaries her mother takes down barehanded, Lucy is forced to confront a lifetime's worth of questions, lies, and betrayal plus master an explosive newfound power all her own.

ISBN: 978-0989105651 *246 pages

For six months after saving the world *again,* Jason Champion stopped threats with little problems. Until the night of a massive explosion where he encounters a shadowy bomber who passes on the chance to kill him.

But Jason's problems kick into high gear when the bomber resurfaces with actions that point to a deadlier endgame. Powerless and broken by a murder he cannot remember committing, Jason must reconsider his alliances and strategy in order to survive a new threat who is out for blood.

ISBN: 978-0989105668* Paperback * 294 pages

Available in paperback and electronic format at www.amazon.com

www.authorbrianthompson.com

BOOK THREE OF THE REJECT HIGH SERIES

FORGOTTEN

BRIAN THOMPSON

Months after absorbing a nuclear explosion, Jason Champion is recuperating in a hospital when he is attacked by a shape-shifter with an agenda. She wants to harvest Jason's radioactive blood to keep his enemy alive.

Following a narrow escape, Jason is joined by his new girlfriend Rhapsody, his ex Sasha, and a new friend, Esteban. While the provenance emerald, scarlet emerald, goshenite, heliodor, and morganite crystals that grant them mysterious powers are safe, there is a new threat.

ISBN: 978-0989105644* Paperback * 300 pages

Available in paperback and electronic format at www.amazon.com

www.authorbrianthompson.com

The school year ending with Reject High's destruction was enough for Jason Champion.

That is until a mysterious new enemy is possessed with the belief that whoever absorbs the radiation will become immortal.

With no other options and their enemies drawing closer to their goal, Jason and a group that has guarded the origin of their power for a century. Its members think the storm will cause an explosion killing millions.

ISBN: 978-0-989-10563-7 * Paperback *258 pages

Available in paperback and electronic format at www.amazon.com

www.authorbrianthompson.com

After his latest fight, Jason Champion is sent to a rundown alternative school, nicknamed "Reject High."

Rhapsody Lowe shows Jason a crystal that turns her invisible. Jason tries one on and he jumps over a city.

With eleven days until Reject High is destroyed, Jason and his friends must dodge their pursuers and save their power source from falling into the wrong hands.

ISBN: 978-0-989-10560-6 * Paperback * 270 pages

www.authorbrianthompson.com

After a failed coup, a revolutionary named Noor is exiled to earth and sentenced to death. He vows to rule the inferior planet.

In the year 2050, tragedy strikes Harper Lowe, Damario Coley, Quinne Ruiz, and Teanna Kirkwood. Through the Genesis Institute, they are all offered the chance to "begin again."

When the project's true motives are revealed, the group is sent hurtling toward an uncertain future with unpredictable consequences.

ISBN: 978-0-615-60216-1 * Paperback * 264 pages

Available in paperback and electronic format at www.amazon.com

www.authorbrianthompson.com

978 0 9 8 9 1 0 5 6 7 5